DEATH RIDES THE RANGE

DEATH RIDES THE RANGE

by

Arthur Henry Gooden

The Golden West Large Print Books
Long Preston, North Yorkshire,
BD23 4ND, England.

British L ~~Cataloguing in Publication Data.~~

Gooden, ~~Arthur Henry~~
D ~~eath rides the range~~

A ~~catalogue record of this book is~~
a~~vailable from the British Library~~

ISBN   978-1-84262-944-4 pbk

First published in Great Britain in 1961
by The Western Book Club

Copyright © Arthur Henry Gooden 1961

Cover illustration © Michael Thomas

The moral right of the author has been asserted

Published in Large Print 2014 by arrangement with
Golden West Literary Agency

The Golden West Large Print is an imprint of Library Magna Books Ltd.

Printed and bound in Great Britain by
T.J. (International) Ltd., Cornwall, PL28 8RW

To

Edith

CHAPTER ONE

Mark Hudson studied the clouds piling above the mountains. A chance for rain, he hoped. The range was parched after a too-long drought. From where he stood on the veranda he could see intermittent flares of lightning, hear the rumble of distant thunder.

Something else sounded sharp above the thunder – the unmistakable report of a rifle. Mark's swift step took him behind one of the massive timbers supporting the veranda roof.

A brief stillness, followed by the quick beat of shod hoofs as the wound-be-killer fled. Mark leaped down the steps and ran to the garden gate in time to glimpse horse and rider disappearing into the dry-wash of the creek beyond the corrals. It was impossible to recognise the man in the fleeting moment, except that he wore what looked like a red calf-skin vest.

Angered by the attempt to shoot him down on his own steps, Mark returned to the veranda and stared frowningly at the place where the bullet had gouged deep into the post. The man had shot too high. A few inches lower and the bullet would have taken him between the eyes.

An elderly Mexican woman appeared, alarm in her eyes.

'What is it?' she asked. 'I heard a gun–'

'It was nothing, probably one of the boys fooling with a rifle.'

His attempts to reassure her failed. She had noticed his scrutiny of the veranda post and in another moment was standing by his side, forefinger touching the scar.

'It is fresh, a bullet hole,' she worried. She turned wide, startled eyes on him. 'Somebody tried to kill you!'

'You have too much imagination, Teresa,' he told her affectionately. 'Always thinking something dreadful is going to happen to me.'

She was studying him with troubled eyes. 'You do not fool me,' she said.

The young cowman smiled, gestured at the distant thunder-heads. 'Rain coming,' he prophesied.

'You are trying to change the subject,' Teresa said vexedly. 'I have known you since the day you were born. I cannot help but worry when your life is in danger.'

'Who told you my life's in danger?' Mark's attention was now on a dust-haze lazily crawling along the road in the chaparral beyond the creek. Somebody was coming from town. He reached for a pair of binoculars lying on a bench near the veranda wall.

'Fidel told me,' Teresa was saying. 'Somebody cut your saddle-girth when you were in town last week. You could have been killed.'

'Fidel talks too much.' Mark levelled the binoculars at the dust-haze. Three riders, too far to make out who they were.

Teresa's tongue was still busy. 'You try to make me think there is nothing wrong, but I know you too well. You are like your father, the old *Señor*. He was always fighting for law and order.'

'All the more reason for me to carry on,' Mark told her.

'You are the image of the old *Señor*–' Her voice grew reproachful. 'When he was your age he had a son – you, to carry on his name, care for this big rancho when he was gone. You should marry – have a son.'

'Plenty of time for that,' Mark said, his binoculars still levelled at the riders. He was able to recognise them, now. Sheriff Corter, and Ed Starkey of the Lazy S. The third

11

man was Reeve Bett, a speculator in land and cattle. Mark's face hardened. He had no liking for the man or his dubious activities in the town.

Teresa's aggrieved voice continued to distract his thoughts. 'I remember the old *Señor's* words the day you were born. He told Fernando to climb into the tower and pull on the rope. "Let the bell ring for my new son," he said.' The Mexican woman wiped moist eyes. 'I want to let the bell ring for *your* son, Markito.'

'I must find a wife, first,' Mark reminded her.

'Lucy Swan would make you a good wife. She is strong and healthy and would bear you fine sons.'

'I've an idea Ross Chaine is sweet on Lucy,' Mark said.

'She's crazy about you!' Teresa scolded. 'But no, you waste your time with that Ellen Brice girl whose father is a cow thief.'

'We don't know that Brice is a cow thief,' Mark said curtly.

'I hear the talk about him,' Teresa persisted, ignoring Mark's frown. 'Because you are in love with the Brice girl you choose to close your ears.'

'You talk nonsense.' Mark replaced the

binoculars on the bench. 'I think we're due for company,' he added.

Sheriff Corter led the way up the veranda steps and sank with a gusty sigh into a chair. 'Glad we found you home, Mark,' he said. He was a tall, lanky man, and the high cheek bones of his darkly-weathered face hinted of a touch of Indian blood.

'A few minutes later and you'd have found me gone,' Mark said. 'I told Pat Race I'd meet him at the Willow Creek camp and I'm due there now.' His welcoming smile took in the sheriff's companions, a friendly smile that concealed his displeasure of Reeve Bett's presence. 'Make yourselves comfortable. Teresa will be out with a pot of coffee.'

Starkey and Bett found chairs while the sheriff's voice rumbled on. 'Our business won't be keeping you long, Mark.'

Ed Starkey was looking with a cowman's interest at the distant thunder-heads. 'We're in for a big rain,' he said, a deep thankfulness in his voice. He was a large, heavy man with pale blue eyes in a beefy red face. 'She'll be a life-saver, Mark. My cows are down to skin and bones.'

'The creeks will be flooding the range,' prophesied Reeve Bett. 'The drought is over, my friends.'

13

'Like I said, our business won't keep you too long from meeting Pat Race,' Sheriff Corter was rumbling. 'Ed and me figgers we got to do something about these rustlers that's plaguin' the San Carlos Country. We've been having a pow-wow with Bett and he thinks he knows where this gang of cow thieves holes up.'

'He knows more than I do,' Mark said. 'What do you want me to do about it?'

'It's like this, Mark,' interrupted Ed Starkey. 'We plan to organise a sort of cowman's vigilante outfit.'

Mark shook his head. 'Leave me out of it.' He looked at the sheriff. 'It's up to you to hunt down these rustlers, Corter.' His voice hardened. 'While you're about it, you can find the man who tried to kill me less than half an hour ago.'

The sheriff reddened. 'I'm not here to listen to fool jokes.'

'No joke,' Mark said. He told them about the rifle shot – showed them the bullet hole.

'It's true,' Teresa told them excitedly. 'I heard the shot! It's God's mercy he was not killed.'

'Did you see the feller, Mark?' asked the sheriff.

Something, perhaps the odd tenseness of

14

Starkey and Reeve Bett as they waited for his answer, made Mark suddenly reluctant to mention the would-be killer's red calf-skin vest, the black and white pinto horse.

'He got away too fast,' he said.

'He could have been one of this rustler's gang,' suggested Starkey. 'It proves our point, Mark. We've got to organise and wipe 'em out.'

'I'm still saying it's the law's business to hunt down these rustlers.' Mark looked at Reeve Bett. 'The sheriff says you know where the gang hides out.'

'That's right,' Bett said. 'I've already passed on my information to Corter.'

'What do you think, Sheriff?' asked Mark. 'Is the law too weak in this man's country to throw some rustlers in jail?'

'I ain't liking your tone,' fumed the sheriff. 'Sounds like you're saying I ain't got the nerve no more.'

'Bett says he told you where these rustlers hide out,' Mark reminded him. 'Why don't you swear in a posse and go after them?'

Ed Starkey got out of his chair. 'We're wasting time,' he grumbled.

'Just a minute, Ed,' rumbled the sheriff. He got to his feet, hitched at sagging gun-belt. 'It's Bett's notion this rustler gang hides out some place close to your Bar H.' The lawman's voice took on an edge. 'You can maybe guess what I'm trying to tell you, Mark.'

'If you mean Brice, you're crazy,' Mark said. He looked resentfully at Reeve Bett.

'I've been checking on stories about him.' Bett put a match to his cigar. 'His ranch lies along the border – a maze of canyons, ideal for a rustlers' roost.'

'That's no proof he's a cow thief,' Mark said angrily.

Sheriff Corter's gaunt face wore a doubtful look. 'Maybe you're right, Mark. Maybe we're barkin' up the wrong tree.' He went dejectedly down the steps, spurs rasping.

Mark watched while they got their horses and rode from the yard. He was aware of a growing uneasiness in him. Something was wrong.

Teresa appeared again. Mark turned to her, asked abruptly, 'Why don't you like Starkey?'

Teresa hesitated, her expression thoughtful. 'He is too friendly with that Bett man,' she finally answered. 'A man who is a good friend of his cannot be an honest man.'

'How do you know Starkey is such a good friend of Bett's?' asked Mark.

'I hear the talk.'

'From Fidel, I suppose.'

'Fidel tells me what he hears in town,' Teresa said, a hint of defiance in her voice. 'Fidel is my grandson. It is right for him to tell me things.'

'I must talk to him,' Mark said.

'Fidel is very smart,' asserted his grandmother. 'He says a good dog does not run with a wolf, which is why I do not like Starkey.'

Fidel saw his boss approaching. He disappeared inside the barn, reappeared with Mark's horse, saddled and bridled.

'You are late for the Willow Creek camp, *Señor*,' he greeted. 'I have had Mingo waiting for you.'

Mark swung into the saddle, held the impatient horse at a standstill, gaze fixed on the young Mexican. 'Did you happen to hear a rifle shot a little while ago?'

'*Si*.' Fidel nodded. 'I was in the barn and thought it was you, *Señor*. The outfit is at Willow Creek camp. Nobody else here to be shooting a gun.'

'Somebody took a shot at me,' Mark informed him. 'The man got away too fast for me to get a look at him. He was riding a black and white pinto.'

17

Fidel's face took on a shocked look. *'Madre de Dios,'* he whispered. 'I will keep a sharp watch for this horse.'

'You have many friends in Old Town,' Mark said. 'You can ask them to keep a sharp look-out, too. I could not see the rider's face. He wore what looked like a red calf-skin vest.'

Fidel nodded, his face sober. 'Leave it to me, *Señor*. I will arrange for many eyes and ears to be on watch.'

'Thanks.' Mark continued to rein the horse in. 'You know those men who came to see me, don't you?'

'*Si–*'

'What do you think of Reeve Bett?'

Fidel hesitated, then read encouragement in Mark's eyes. 'I hear bad things about him.'

'What kind of bad things?'

'I hear talk in Old Town he hires men with guns to kill for him,' Fidel said in a low voice. 'He wears a smile, but his heart is black.'

'Your grandmother says you do not like Starkey because he is Bett's friend.'

'It is true, *Señor*,' admitted the young Mexican. 'I do not trust any man who is a friend of *Señor* Bett.'

'You talk good sense, Fidel,' approved

Mark. 'I'm giving your job to old Tulsa.'

Fidel turned pale. 'You – you mean I – I'm fired?' he stammered.

'I have a better job for you.'

With relief, the young Mexican waited for Mark to continue.

'Starting today, you draw top-hand pay as a full-time member of the Bar H outfit,' Mark said.

'*Gracias!*' Fidel's face glowed. 'I will make you a good *vaquero*. I love this old rancho where I was born.'

'It's a very special job I have in mind for you at this time.' Mark paused, his expression suddenly doubtful. 'It could be dangerous, Fidel.'

The young Mexican's hand lifted in a gesture that brushed aside any thought of danger. 'It is nothing – this danger.'

Mark studied him attentively, and liked what he saw. Teresa's grandson was amply endowed with intelligence and courage – and loyalty.

'You can help me a lot if you go to San Carlos and keep your eyes and ears open.'

'I can stay at the *cantina* of my Uncle Juan in Old Town,' Fidel suggested.

'Fine.' Mark nodded approval. He knew and trusted Juan Moraga.

'I will do my best,' Fidel said simply. There was pride, and dignity in the lift of his head.

Mark continued to hold the restive buckskin at a standstill. He was more and more conscious of a driving urge to get to the Brice ranch. The recent accusations against Brice worried him. Brice was Ellen's father; the danger that menaced him included the girl.

He came to a decision. 'Fidel – throw a saddle on your horse. I want you to ride over to Willow Creek and tell Pat Race I won't be out there today.' He was scribbling on the back of an envelope as he spoke. 'I've got to get out to the Brice ranch in a hurry and it may be late before I'm back. Here's a note for Jim Stagg.'

Fidel took the pencilled envelope and put it carefully in his shirt pocket. 'You want me to go to San Carlos today?' he asked.

'That's right,' Mark said. 'Just as soon as you can make it from Willow Creek.' Mark lifted the reins. '*Adios,*' he called over his shoulder. 'Good luck, and watch your step.'

CHAPTER TWO

Mark was doing some hard thinking as he rode across the mesa. He could not shake off the impression that Starkey and Bett had some connection with the attempt on his life. Their furtive interest when the sheriff asked if he had seen the ambusher, their ill-concealed relief at his reply, worried him.

The trail dipped down to the dry bed of a creek fringed with cottonwoods. Normally there was always a small stream flowing here. The drought had left only a sandy wash. Mark glanced hopefully at the distant thunderheads. When the rain finally came, the sandy wash would become a turbulent flood – a living creek again.

Presently the cliffs drew apart. The trail began a zigzag descent of a rugged, boulder-strewn slope.

Mark halted the horse, gazed thoughtfully down at the small white house that stood by a creek and was half hidden by huge cotton-woods. A buckboard stood near the barn, and several horses were nosing at a straw pile in the corral. All very neat, and shrieking of newness. Samuel Brice's ranch home.

Troubled speculation clouded Mark's eyes as he studied the scene below. There was a mystery about Brice, a mystery Mark felt had nothing to do with cattle rustlers. The talk linking him with rustlers was a deliberate and vicious plot to ruin Brice – frighten him from the country, or worse still, put a rope around his neck.

There was nothing of the cowman about Brice. Speech and manner betrayed him for an Easterner, a tall, quiet-voiced scholarly man. A college professor, perhaps; a lawyer, a doctor, but never a cow thief. Some tragedy had driven Brice to seek a new home in the remote wilds of the Southwest.

He rode around a massive upthrust of granite and the house came into view again. A girl appeared from the kitchen door. She paused on the steps, a slim figure in white. Ellen Brice, and at the sight of her, Mark was conscious of a stir within him. He knew she was the real reason for this hasty trip. She was more than just Brice's daughter. She was the girl he loved.

She turned and looked across the yard at the barn. Brice emerged from the stable, leading a harnessed team of horses. The girl waved a hand at him, then vanished inside the kitchen. Brice led the team towards the buckboard.

The trail looped again behind a series of great boulders that cut off further view of the ranch yard. The last turn showed Brice backing the team to the buckboard. It also revealed a newcomer on the scene, a man, crouched behind a clump of greasewood, a rifle levelled in his hands.

Mark's warning shout was too late. Even as he sent the buckskin on the dead run across the flats he heard the sharp report of the rifle, saw Brice stagger, collapse. Although the distance was too great for his .45, Mark flung two futile shots as the man disappeared in the concealing willows of the nearby creek.

Ellen was running from the house when Mark pulled to a standstill near the corral. She sank on her knees by her father's prone body, gave Mark a horrified look as he hurried up, the forgotten gun still clutched in his fingers.

'You murderer!' Loathing was in her voice. 'You've killed my father!'

Mark shook his head. 'No, Ellen, I didn't do this.' He dropped to his knees by her side, gently fingered Brice's limp wrist. He muttered a relieved exclamation.

'I can feel a pulse... He's not dead!'

Ellen watched in silence while he continued his examination, relief and contrition in her eyes as he told her about the man with the rifle.

'He got away too fast for a look at him. No time to chase him ... I had to get to your father as quickly as possible on the chance that he was still alive.'

'I – I'm sorry ... I should have know you – you couldn't have done it.'

'You heard the shots, saw me running up with a gun in my hand,' Mark said. 'What else could you think?'

'I shouldn't have doubted you.' Ellen sprang to her feet. 'I'll get something for a bandage.' She sped away to the house.

Ellen was soon back with strips of linen, a sponge and a pail of water. Mark gently cleaned the wound and adjusted a temporary bandage. The girl was on her knees again, anxious eyes on her father's pale face.

'He's coming out of it,' Mark said. 'He's going to be all right.'

Brice's eyes fluttered open, met their relieved looks. 'What happened?' His eyes closed again.

'Somebody took a shot at you,' Mark told

him. 'You're lucky.'

Brice's eyes opened wide now, a wry smile in them. 'I don't feel so lucky.' He looked at Ellen. 'It's all right ... Mark is here now.'

'Let's get you to the house,' Mark said. 'Do you think you can make it.'

'I can try,' Brice said. 'Feeling better every minute.'

They got him to his feet and into his bedroom. Brice stretched out on the bed and stared frowningly at his bandaged shoulder. 'I seem to have enemies, Mark.'

'I'm afraid you're right,' Mark said.

'It's worse than you know,' Brice told him. 'Feel in the pocket of that shirt.'

Mark's fingers explored the pocket, extracted a crumpled sheet of coarse brown paper. He read the scrawl, pencilled in large capital letters. GET OUT OR BE BURNT OUT.

'I found it pinned on the stable door this morning,' Brice said. 'I'm not telling Ellen, yet.'

Mark tossed the shirt aside, his fascinated gaze on the grim warning. 'Yes,' he said. 'You're right. It's worse than I suspected. Somebody took a shot at me this morning. Missed me by a short inch, and then I had callers, Sheriff Corter and Ed Starkey of the

Lazy S, and Reeve Bett.'

'Reeve Bett,' muttered Brice. 'I don't like him, Mark. He was out here last week, asking too many questions; and worse still, he made eyes at Ellen. I told him to get out and not to come back.'

'He's spreading the story that you're a rustler,' Mark said. 'He's got Sheriff Corter believing him. The thing worried me. I told them they were crazy and as soon as they left I rode over to warn you.' Mark shook his head regretfully. 'I got here too late.'

'I've got to talk with the sheriff,' he said. 'Corter should know I'm not a cow thief.'

Mark had been doing some fast thinking. He shook his head. 'You and Ellen are not staying here.'

'What do you mean?' Brice frowned over his cup. 'This is our home. I'm not letting them frighten me away.'

'You've got to think of Ellen. This place is too lonesome. Anything could happen. They'll be trying again.'

The colour drained from the older man's face. 'Ellen,' he muttered. 'Yes – I've got to think of Ellen.'

'She won't leave here unless you go, too,' Mark said. His fingers tightened over the piece of crumpled paper in his pocket. 'The warning means all it says.'

'Where can we go?' Brice asked the question despairingly.

'I'm taking you back to the ranch. You'll be safe there.'

'My cattle – the horses?'

'We'll take the horses with us. I'll have Pat Race throw the cattle in with my herd.' Mark paused, added grimly, 'We've got to tell Ellen the truth.'

'I suppose you're right,' Brice said dejectedly.

Their eyes went to the girl, hastening in with a pan of warm water and towels.

'You're looking better already,' she said.

Mark drew the piece of brown paper from his pocket and laid it on the bed. 'You tell her,' he said to Brice. 'I'll be rounding up your team.'

The girl's look followed him until he disappeared through the door, then slowly she reached for the piece of paper. She smoothed it, read the scrawled words aloud, 'Get out or be burnt out.'

Her face paled. 'Father! What does it mean?'

'I'm afraid it means just what it says, Ellen.'

Ellen stood rigid for a moment, then with

a defiant gesture she flung the paper to the floor and turned to the basin of water. 'Right now I'm going to clean you up,' she said.

Brice gave her a fond look, and while she sponged his blood-stained side he told her of Mark's plan to take them back to his ranch. She listened, wordless, trouble deepening in her eyes.

Lightning flared at the windows, thunder growled and rumbled. Ellen's head listed. 'Listen,' she said. 'Rain – it's beginning to rain.'

CHAPTER THREE

It was in Ellen's mind that she would never forget the journey through the pelting rain to Mark Hudson's ranch. Her father by her side in the ranch wagon, they moved slowly under dripping black clouds. Mark had insisted upon their immediate departure. He said their enemies would not be watching the roads in such a storm, which was really a boon, helping to cover their escape.

Although he was thankful for the needed rain, Mark could not help wishing the storm had held off for an hour or two. The narrow road was rapidly becoming more and more perilous. It would be easy for the light wagon to slide over the precipice into the rushing waters of the creek a hundred feet below.

Other thoughts vexed his mind. The identify of Brice's would-be killer. His brief search, while rounding up the team had failed to disclose any clues. Only a few cigarette butts where the man had been crouching behind the greasewood bush, waiting for his murderous attempt.

Mark forced his thoughts back to the more immediate dangers of the storm-bound road. The problem now was to get Ellen and her wounded father safely to the ranch.

He found the place he wanted, where the road was wide enough for the wagon to draw alongside. He got down from his saddle. Ellen halted the team and peered apprehensively at him through the rain.

'What is it?' Her voice was almost lost in the roar of the torrential downpour. She sat stiffly upright on the wagon seat, reins clutched in both hands, dripping oilskin buttoned under her chin.

'I'm driving the rest of the way,' Mark said.

'I was getting frightened,' she admitted.

They reached the floor of the canyon. Mark kept the team moving as fast as safety allowed. The place could be a death trap. Already his straining ears heard ominous sounds. The inevitable cloudburst had struck the higher reaches of the canyon, was hurling its turbulent flood downstream with the speed of a racing horse. He had seen the havoc wrought by those irresistible floods, trees uprooted, great boulders tossed like chips.

Ellen and Brice now heard the deep-toned

roar of the flood waters. The girl's arm tightened around her father, her face turned in a frightened look at Mark, grimly intent on keeping the swaying wagon upright. She saw his lips move, faintly heard his shouted words. 'Another hundred yards.'

They reached the turn of the road and started up the grade. The climb dragged the team to a slow walk. Mark was content. Another sharp turn brought them to a bluff some hundred feet above the canyon floor. He halted the team, pushed the reins into Ellen's hands.

'Wait here, while I scout up the road.'

'What is it?' she asked, alarmed to see him reach for the holstered gun under his slicker.

'I don't know, but I'm taking a look.' He slid over the wheel and vanished into the brush.

'A deer, perhaps, or a bear,' Brice said.

Ellen shook her head. 'No, not a deer, not a bear. A man. Mark thinks there's a man, somewhere close.'

Brice was silent. He knew she was right. It was entirely possible the killer had taken refuge from the storm under some boulders, had spotted them and was now crouching in ambush.

The stillness seemed unearthly now the

rain had stopped. No sound to tell them where Mark could be, betray him to a possible enemy. Suddenly the stillness was blasted by a rifle shot, then again only the hushed roar of the creek, the murmuring rills. Ellen's heart stood still. She gave her father a stricken look, started to wrap the reins around the brake.

Brice said, 'Sit still ... he told us to wait here.'

'He needs help ... I want your gun–'

'You would only make things worse for him,' Brice said.

'I suppose you're right.' Ellen reluctantly reached for the reins. Her nerves were tingling.

Mark had worked his way through the brush to a point some three hundred feet up the road where it looped to the left. He lay prone behind a boulder where he had flung himself when his unseen quarry had taken the pot-shot at him. Smoke curled from behind a big boulder visible just beyond the bend of the road. The bullet had screamed past him, too close for comfort.

Moments passed, grew to minutes. Slowly a head showed above the boulder. After a cautious look, the ambusher stood upright, rifle in hands. It was obvious he thought his bullet had found its target. He took a step forward, another step towards where he guessed his victim was lying dead in the brush.

Mark lay very still, watching the man. Only his booted feet showed, his fallen hat. He wanted the man to get close enough, within range of the .45 in his hand.

For another long minute the killer stood motionless, rifle held ready for instant action. The boots, the limp, half-seen legs – the fallen hat, seemed to reassure him. A satisfied grin creased his lips, and suddenly he was moving swiftly.

Mark nerved himself to wait until less than ten feet separated them. With a quick twist he was on his feet, gun levelled.

'Hold it,' he said.

The man's rifle lifted, fell from his hands as Mark fired. He stared with horrified eyes at Mark, blood dripping from a shattered hand.

'Turn round,' Mark said. 'Down – flat on your face.'

The man obeyed. Mark picked up the fallen rifle.

'Keep very still,' he warned. 'One stir, and the next bullet goes through your head.'

'I ain't stirrin',' muttered the man.

Down the road, below the bend, Ellen and her father had heard the second shot.

'Mark's gun,' Brice guessed. 'His .45 ... the first was a rifle.'

They heard Mark's voice, calling for Ellen to bring the wagon. She released the brake, started the team, and they went on up the grade.

Mark, watchfully close to the captive, motioned for her to halt in the bend of the road. She braked the wagon to a standstill, gazed wide-eyed at the prostrate man, the blood-smeared shattered hand.

'Good work, Mark,' Brice said. 'I'm hoping he's the scoundrel who tried to kill me.'

'We'll know when I get a look under his slicker,' Mark said. 'His horse must be cached somewhere near. If it's a black and white pinto I'll know we've got the man who took a shot at me this morning.'

Ellen found her voice. 'What are you going to do with him?'

'You'll find some rope under the tarpaulin,' Mark told her.

She tied the reins to the brake, climbed from the wagon and rummaged under the canvas sheet for the requested rope. She handed it to Mark, colour in her cheeks at the warmth in his eyes, the squeeze of his fingers over hers.

'You might look up the road for the horse he's cached in the brush,' he said.

Ellen glanced at the sun, now hot in the western sky. 'I'm shedding this rain-coat first.' She stripped off the slicker, tossed it into the wagon.

'My hand's hurtin' like hell,' moaned the man. 'You figger to leave me bleed to death?'

'Don't worry,' Mark said. 'I'm saving you for the hangman.' Using the prisoner's bandanna, he improvised a bandage and tied his hands behind his back with a piece of cord.

'You can get up now,' he ordered.

The man got awkwardly to his feet. Mark ripped his slicker open, disclosed a red calf-skin vest.

'You're the man who took that shot at me this morning,' he said.

'Ain't never seen you before in my life,' denied the desperado. He was a slight, swarthy man, obviously of mixed blood and none of it good.

'You tried to kill Mr Brice in his own yard,' Mark accused him. 'You were planning an ambush here.'

'You're crazy,' snarled the man. 'All I done was take cover from the storm in them rocks yonder ... figgered you was a bear or some-

35

thin', sneakin' up on me.'

Ellen's voice drew Mark's attention. She had a black and white pinto in tow. 'I found him behind a clump of junipers,' she called.

Mark turned back to his prisoner. 'That's the horse I saw this morning, and you and your red calfskin vest were in the saddle. No use lying.'

'I ain't talkin'.'

'What's your name?'

'Ain't talkin'.'

Mark untied his wrists, motioned at the pinto with his gun. 'Climb your saddle.'

The man obeyed. Mark retied his wrists to the saddlehorn and lashed his feet to the stirrups.

'You won't be keepin' me long,' the man said with a pain-distorted grin. 'My boss'll nail your hide to your barn door.'

Mark ignored the threat. 'Get my horse,' he said to Ellen.

She brought the buckskin from the rear of the wagon. Mark swung into his saddle, waited for her to climb back to her seat. She pulled off her hat and tossed it on the tarpaulin behind her, sat eagerly erect, wind-riffled hair touched with golden lights under the westering sun.

'Let's go!' She gave Mark a bright-eyed

look. 'You lead – we follow.'

The sun was a shimmering disc on the western peaks when they came in sight of the Hudson ranch house. The roar of rushing flood waters had faded into the distance. The storm was over.

CHAPTER FOUR

The Hudson ranch house had grown to a large rambling dwelling since Mark's father had settled in the San Carlos Country at the close of the Mexican War. The original log and adobe structure now formed one of the wings enclosing the patio and was the undisputed domain of Teresa Cota. It was here the Mexican servants had their quarters, and what was formerly the living-room was now a huge kitchen floored with worn red adobe bricks.

It was in a dim corner of the old kitchen, under colourful strings of dangling chilli peppers that Teresa's venerable father, Fernando, spent most of his hours, nodding drowsily or rolling endless little brown paper cigarettes.

Teresa joined him, stood silent for a moment, looking at the driving rain. She turned troubled eyes on her father. 'I do not like it,' she said.

'It is good – this rain,' Fernando told her.

'I am thinking of Markito,' Teresa said. 'I

do not like him going off to the Brice ranch the way he did.' She shook her head gloomily. 'I do not like this attempt to kill Markito this morning.'

Fernando's fingers were busy with cigarette paper and tobacco.

'You are foolish to worry.' His voice was surprisingly sonorous. 'You must trust our young *Señor* always. He has the mind and courage of his father. Do not fear for him.'

'I can't help but worry,' Teresa said. 'That Brice girl has bewitched him. I'm not fooled by his talk. He is in love with her, a daughter of a cow thief, it is said.'

Fernando shook his head. 'Do not believe such tales of the girl's father,' he admonished. 'Our young *Señor* would not love the daughter of a cow thief. If he loves her it is proof that *Señor* Brice is an honest man.'

'You are so wise,' Teresa said. Her head turned in a look at the young Mexican woman running into the kitchen. 'What is it, Delfina?'

'Somebody comes – a young girl, struggling on foot through the storm?'

'Who is she?'

'I could not see her face for the rain,' Delfina said. 'She lies on the front steps.'

Teresa uttered an exclamation, went

swiftly from the kitchen and down the long hall to the front door. She flung it open, stood for a moment, peering through the downpour, the Mexican girl at her side.

'*Señorita!*' Teresa ran across the veranda and down to the lower step, heedless of the rain that immediately drenched her to the skin. She bent over the girl lying there, gestured frantically for Delfina to help her.

'Quick – it is the *Señorita* Swan!'

They pulled the girl to her feet; an elderly Mexican woman ran to them from the hall, and the three of them half dragged, half carried their limp burden into the hall. Delfina slammed the door shut while Teresa bent anxiously over the girl.

'*Señorita* – poor little one ... this is terrible!' The housekeeper snatched a towel from the elderly Mexican woman and gently wiped the splatters of mud from the girl's face.

Lucy Swan opened her eyes, looked up dazed at the kindly face bent over her. 'I – I thought I'd die.' She sat up, put both hands to her face and began to cry. 'Oh, Teresa. It's dreadful... Dad was shot and killed in town early this morning! I was coming to tell Mark – ask him to help.'

Horror filled Teresa's eyes. 'You poor little

one,' she repeated.

'I got caught in this awful storm,' the girl told her shocked listeners. 'I was almost here, in the avenue, when lightning hit us, killed my mare and knocked me senseless for a few minutes. It was dreadful! I thought I'd drown before I got here, crawling through the mud.'

'Quick, Petra – a hot drink,' Teresa said to the older woman.

'*Si–*' The cook scurried off to her kitchen.

'We're getting you out of those wet clothes and into a nice warm bed,' Teresa said. 'Help me, Delfina.'

Propped against the pillows, Lucy sipped the hot coffee. 'You're so good, Teresa,' she said gratefully.

'Thank the good saints you got here!' Teresa touched the little silver cross at her bosom.

'I want to see Mark,' Lucy Swan said. 'Isn't Mark here, Teresa?'

'No, *Señorita.*'

Lucy's dark eyes widened at the curt answer, the sudden tightening of Teresa's lips.

'Where is he?' she asked.

'Only God knows,' Teresa said harshly, then concerned at the quick alarm in the dark eyes she added more gently, 'Do not worry, *Señor-*

ita. No doubt he has taken refuge from the storm and will be home soon.'

The answer seemed to satisfy the girl. She finished the coffee, sank back on the pillows and attempted to smile. 'I'm feeling not so shaky. It has all been so dreadful – father – murdered – the storm–'

The evening shadows were crawling when Mark turned into the avenue with his prisoner, Ellen trailing him with the wagon. He reined to a quick standstill, gazed wonderingly at the dead mare partially blocking the drive.

Uneasy premonitions disturbed him as he recognised Lucy Swan's bay mare – her silver-mounted saddle – the silver-embossed bridle. No sign of the girl, and no footprints in the drying mud. The heavy rain would have washed them away.

Ellen drew up with the wagon and she and Brice gazed with startled eyes at the dead animal.

'Killed by lightning,' Brice guessed. 'The rider must have escaped.'

Ellen, watching Mark, saw the frowning recognition in his eyes – his growing dismay. 'Would it be one of your own men?' she asked.

'No,' Mark replied. 'Not one of my riders.'

'You seemed to recognise the horse,' Ellen said.

Mark chose to ignore her question. 'There's just room to crowd past if you pull off the road a little,' he said.

Ellen started the team and managed to crowd past and back into the road. The team was too weary to be frightened of the dead animal. The horses trailing on the lead-rope were snorting reluctant until Mark urged them on with his quirt.

Another quarter of a mile brought them to the ranch yard. They splashed across pools of water to the barn. Mark slid from his saddle, stood for a moment, gazing through the dusk at the house. Lucy Swan had apparently escaped the fate of her mare. There was only one place she could be – in the house. He wondered why she should have ventured to come in such a storm. And now she and Ellen Brice would be together under one roof – his roof. The uneasy premonitions mounted in him.

Only an ominous stillness in the big yard. No sign of Tulsa – no answer to his shout. New dismay filled him. It was apparent that Tulsa had not arrived from the Willow Creek camp, delayed probably by the storm, or perhaps Fidel Cota had himself been storm-bound and unable to deliver his message to Pat Race. Perhaps Tulsa and Fidel were both dead, caught in a cloudburst. The disturbing thoughts chased through his mind while he was unloading his bound prisoner from his saddle.

'Just a few minutes while I get this man stowed away in a safe place,' he said to Ellen and Brice who were climbing from the wagon seat.

He pushed the sullen prisoner towards a small, disused granary. The building had stout adobe walls with windows little more than air-vents. He pulled the door open and motioned with his gun.

'You ain't holdin' me long,' the desperado said as he stepped inside. 'I've got friends.'

Mark slammed the heavy door shut and slid the bar. Later, he would get a padlock from the office and secure the bar from outside interference.

He hurried back to the wagon. Ellen was unhooking the exhausted team, Brice helping with his uninjured hand.

'The poor things are about dead,' commiserated the girl.

Mark opened the stable door; she led the horses inside to a stall. Mark followed with his buckskin and the pinto, hastened out for the horses tied to the wagon. When he led them into the stable, Ellen was throwing hay down to the mangers.

'You shouldn't be doing that,' he remonstrated.

'I want to help, and there seems to be nobody around.'

Mark climbed over the manger and took the fork from her. 'I'll finish it,' he said. 'You can be getting some of your things from the wagon. We must get your father to the house. He should be in bed and have a fresh bandage on his shoulder.'

He finished forking the hay into the mangers and climbed from the loft. He was tired, too, and he stood for a minute. He then went out to the wagon. Ellen had rummaged two valises from under the tarpaulin and stood waiting by her father's side. Lights gleamed through the growing darkness from the house. Mark picked up the larger of the valises and the three of them started across the yard. They reached the patio gate as the front door flew open, revealed Teresa Cota framed against the lamplight. She uttered an astonished squeal.

'Markito! What – what–' Words failed her. She stood there, transfixed, her mouth open.

'I've brought guests back with me,' Mark

said from the foot of the veranda steps. 'You know them, Teresa.'

'*Si*,' murmured the Mexican woman. 'I – I know them–'

'Mr Brice has been shot – wounded,' Mark told her. 'I want him and Miss Brice to stay with us a few days.'

Teresa reluctantly moved aside for them to enter the hall. Mark turned and looked at her; the sternness in his eyes made her draw in a sharp breath.

'Mr Brice must get to bed at once,' he said. 'Miss Brice, too, should be in bed. She has been through a dreadful ordeal.'

A hint of compassion softened the housekeeper's face as she looked at the weary girl, her mud-splattered clothes. 'Come with me, *Señorita*,' she said. 'I will make you comfortable ... bring you a hot drink.' Innate kindness was fast overcoming her shock. 'Delfina!' she called. 'Come and help.'

The young Mexican girl hastened up the hall. It was obvious she had been watching the scene from the kitchen door. At Teresa's gesture, she took the large valise from Mark.

'Prepare the bed in the big room,' Teresa told her. '*Señor* Brice has been wounded and must rest...'

She took the small valise from Ellen,

46

turned with a beckoning smile, halted as a door opened and Lucy Swan ran into the hall.

The girl paused for a moment, dark eyes wide on Mark. With a little cry she flew to him, high heels tapping, white skirt swirling. 'Mark! Oh, Mark!' Her head nestled against his shoulder. 'I had to come to you! Dad's been shot – killed.' She began to weep. 'Oh, Mark, I nearly died getting here!'

Mark stood petrified, unable to speak. Ellen gazed back at him, her face very pale, a stunned look in her eyes. He met her look, sensed the shock in her. She was seeing the picture all wrong, he thought miserably. She was thinking that Lucy Swan was his sweetheart. In another moment she was following Teresa down the hall.

Mark resisted the impulse to push Lucy aside and run after her. The import of the weeping girl's words were beginning to make sense. *Bill Swan shot ... killed.* He could hardly believe his ears.

'Your – your father – dead?'

'Yes – murdered–' Lucy lifted a tear-stained face. 'It's dreadful, Mark! I'm almost crazy!'

Mark's stunned look went to Brice. The older man was in the last stages of exhaustion and blood was seeping from his bandaged shoulder. There was only one thing he could do at that moment. Attend to Brice, get him into bed and put on a fresh bandage and somehow send for the doctor to extract the bullet still in the shoulder.

'Lucy–' He spoke gently. 'Mr Brice has been seriously hurt. You must wait a few minutes while I look after him.' He led her to the hall sofa. 'There,' he said, as she relaxed on the cushions. 'I'll be with you soon and you can tell me all about it.' He helped Brice down the hall to a door where Delfina stood waiting.

In the other bedroom, Ellen Brice was watching Teresa throw back the covers of the bed. She felt numb, bewildered. Who was the dark-haired girl who seemed to know Mark so intimately, who had flung herself into his arms with the news that her father had been shot and killed?

'Now, *Señorita*,' Teresa said briskly. 'Get out of your damp clothes. I'll fetch you a nightgown.'

Ellen sat on the edge of the bed. 'Who – who is she?' she asked.

'You mean *Señorita* Swan?' When she chose, Teresa could speak English. 'Poor little thing. Her father has just been murdered. She was on her way here to tell Mark when lightning hit her horse. She crawled through the mud to our door about an hour ago – a pitiful sight.'

Teresa quite understood the cause of the girl's agitation, the strained look on her pale face.

'Yes,' she agreed, not looking at Ellen. 'She and our young *Señor* played together when they were children. They are made for each other – those two.' She looked back from the door. 'I will send Delfina with a nightdress.' The door closed behind her.

Ellen continued to sit on the bed. *Made for each other … Mark and the Swan girl were made for each other.* The housekeeper's placid voice was still in her ears, torturing, impossible words. Mark had never mentioned her name, and yet she had seen it with her own eyes – seen the girl clinging to him as if sure of his comfort – his love.

Another thought came to her. The expression on Mark's face was not the pleased anticipation of a man in love. Quite the reverse. She had grown to know Mark better than he knew, could read his thoughts.

Ellen's lips tightened. The Swan girl was not going to take Mark Hudson from her. She would show her a thing or two.

A gentle tap on the door; Delfina came into

the room, a nightgown over an arm. 'Let me 'ave those clothes, *Señorita*,' the Mexican girl said. 'I weel take to the laundry for dry them.'

'Is my father in bed yet?' Ellen asked.

'Si. *Señor* Mark ees mooch worry for heem. *Señor* Mark say must get doctor for take bullet from arm. Nobody to go for doctor. *Señor* mooch worry.'

Ellen got up from the bed. 'Never mind the nightgown,' she said. 'I'm not going to bed now.'

Delfina gazed at her helplessly, the nightgown on her arm. '*Señora* say for you go to bed queek.'

Ellen shook her head, reached for the boots she had slipped off. She was suddenly aware of a new strength in her, the weariness gone. Mark was in need of help and she was going to help, no matter what he said. Her father was in dire need of a doctor and she was going to get that doctor.

'I'm riding to San Carlos for a doctor,' she told the Mexican girl.

'*Señorita!*' gasped Delfina. 'Not in the dark! No safe for you!'

Ellen pulled on the other boot, reached for her damp Stetson. 'Damn the dark,' she said. She hurried from the room.

Delfina watched her go, alarm in her eyes.

She tossed the nightgown on the bed and ran into the hall. She was in time to see Ellen disappear in the adjoining bedroom where Mark was attending to Brice. Shaking her head dubiously, the Mexican girl hurried to the kitchen.

CHAPTER FIVE

Mark was sponging her father's shoulder with a disinfectant when Ellen burst into the room. 'I thought Teresa was putting you to bed,' he said.

'I'm not going to lie in bed when you're needing help.' Her sparkling eyes emphasised the determined lift of her chin.

'What do you mean?' Mark stared at her. 'There's nothing you can do, except rest.'

'I'm riding to San Carlos for a doctor.'

Mark could only look at her. It was her father who broke the brief silence. 'You're crazy,' Brice said from his pillow.

'Mark has nobody here to send for the doctor,' argued the girl. 'You must have a doctor as soon as possible, and so must that man locked in the granary. Delfina heard what Mark said and she told me.' Her mouth tightened mutinously. 'I'm riding to San Carlos now, just as soon as I can get my saddle from the wagon and on my mare.'

'Impossible!' ejaculated Brice.

Ellen looked at Mark busy again with the

sponge. With a defiant lift of her head she turned to the door. Mark's voice stopped her.

'Wait a minute. Let me finish this bandage.'

She gazed back at him from the door. 'You will let me help – go for the doctor?'

His silence held her while he continued to bandage the wound. 'I think that will hold you until the doctor probes for the bullet,' he finally said to Brice. He drew up the light blanket. 'Take it easy, and don't worry about Ellen. We're not letting her go to San Carlos.' He turned to the impatient girl.

'It's not safe for you to go, Ellen, be seen in San Carlos. Anything might happen to you.'

'I know where Dr Brown lives,' Ellen told him. 'Who's going to see me – recognise me in the dark?'

'We can't risk it.' Mark went to her, took her hands in his, held them tight. 'At least, I can't risk it,' he added in a voice so low she hardly heard the words.

The tension went from Ellen, her mutinous mouth softened. She thought of the Swan girl. *He wouldn't use that tone to her ... he wouldn't look at her the way he's looking at me.*

She said, feebly, 'Somebody must go.'

'I'll go, when I've attended to the man in the granary.' His voice hardened. 'There's another reason why you must not risk being seen in town. It must not be known for the present that you and your father are staying here. I want them to think you have obeyed the warning and left the country.'

Ellen again thought of the Swan girl who had come for Mark's help. 'It's too late for that,' she said. 'Miss Swan won't keep the secret long. It will soon be known we're here – with you.'

'Lucy won't tell if I ask her to promise not to.' Dismay clouded Mark's eyes. He dropped Ellen's hands. He was forgetting Lucy Swan, waiting for him in the hall. She had come for his help. Her father had been murdered – Bill Swan, his old friend, murdered. How could he go to San Carlos with Lucy now on his hands?

Ellen read his harassed thoughts. She said, quietly, 'It's no use, Mark. She's needing you, and it means I'm the only one you can send to San Carlos.' She stood before him, slim, determined, compassion, understanding, in her eyes.

'No!' he said, almost violently. 'Let me think!'

The sharp tread of booted feet came up

the hall, paused at the bedroom door. *'Señor!'* A deep, sonorous voice that spun Mark on his heels.

The door pushed open, revealed old Fernando Cota, a smile warming his leathery face. He stood upright, the weight of years flung from massive shoulders, a sombrero on the white mane of his head, gun-belt girding his waist, spurs jingling on boot-heels. Mark gazed at him as if seeing a ghost.

'Fernando!' Mark exclaimed, amazement in his voice. 'What – what–'

'Señor,' interrupted the Mexican. 'Delfina has told us of the young *Señorita's* plan to ride to San Carlos for the doctor. It is not safe for her to ride through the dark night to that bad town.' His benign, admiring smile rested briefly on the girl. 'She is brave, this young *Señorita,* but she must not go. I, Fernando Cota, will go.'

Mark could hardly believe his eyes, his ears. It had been years since the old vaquero had sat a saddle. The hard ride to town might finish him. Before he could give voice to his doubts, Teresa burst into the room, skirts billowing, face pale with fright. It was plain she had heard her father announce his intention of riding to San Carlos.

'No, no, no!' she told him shrilly. 'You are too old to sit a saddle. You will fall off – be killed!' She waved her hands at him. 'Go back to your kitchen chair, old man!'

'Not so!' Fernando smote his chest. 'Tonight I am not old. Tonight I am strong as any bull on the range.' He gestured grandly. 'Tonight I serve our young *Señor* as I served the Old *Señor,* his father, when trouble came to the rancho.'

Mark studied him for a moment. Something had indeed miraculously rekindled the fires in the aged Mexican. He was seeing Fernando as he remembered him in boyhood days, tough, tireless, indomitable – the best ranch foreman his father ever had.

'All right, Fernando,' he said. 'Throw a saddle on a horse and hit the trail for town.'

'*Si, Señor.*'

'It's a long time since you have been in town. You will not know where to find the doctor.'

'No, *Señor*. I will go to the *cantina* of my nephew, Juan Moraga in Old Town. He will take my message to the doctor.'

'Fine!' Mark nodded approval. 'You've got a good head on your shoulders, Fernando.' He paused, added emphatically, 'Don't try to get back to the ranch tonight. You can stay over at the *cantina*.'

Pride replaced the anxiety on Teresa's face. She gave her father fond look. 'Make sure you do what Markito says,' she admonished as she followed him out to the hall.

Ellen went to the door, peered down the hall. She closed the door quietly and looked around at Mark.

'Miss Swan is waiting for you on the sofa,' she said.

Mark picked up the box, reached for the basin, contemplated them frowningly. He had little pity for the wounded desperado, but it was inhuman to let the man suffer too long. His bullet-mangled hand needed attention. Despite his concern about the grieving girl – the news of the tragedy, there was nothing he could immediately do for her. He came to a decision.

'Ellen,' he said, 'you say you want to help me–'

'Yes – yes–'

'Get a lantern from the kitchen and meet me out there in the patio.' He gestured at the side door. 'I'm going out that way because I don't want to see Lucy Swan yet – not until I've had a look at that man in the granary.'

'I understand.' Ellen stepped into the hall, closed the door behind her.

Mark turned back to Brice, met his inquiring look.

'What do you make of it, Mark? This Swan murder?' Brice glanced at his bandaged shoulder. 'Who's responsible for all this shooting?'

'I don't know.' Mark shook his head. 'I wish I knew the answer. Swan was a fine man, one of my best friends.'

'It seems he was marked for murder, too,' Brice said. 'It's very frightening.' He leaned back on his pillows. 'I feel so useless, lying here, and you needing help.'

'Ellen is helping me.'

'She's a grand girl, Mark. You don't half know how fine she is.'

'I'm learning about her fast.' Mark studied the older man's weary face curiously. The shock of the wound, the ride through the storm, had been too much for him. 'Don't worry,' he advised. 'Worry won't help.'

'You don't know much about me, Mark.' The feverish voice rambled on. 'There are things I should tell you – some day – some day–' The voice faded to silence.

Mark saw that he was asleep, and after a moment, he went on noiseless feet through the side door into the patio. He stood there in the dark, wondering about the mystery of

Samuel Brice – the reason that had brought him and Ellen to this remote corner of the Territory of New Mexico. It was evident that Brice suspected he was in love with Ellen, wanted him to know that reason.

Lantern light danced through the darkness, revealed Ellen hurrying towards him.

'Delfina lit it for me,' she said as he took the lantern from her. 'Teresa is with Miss Swan. She is very beautiful, isn't she? Miss Swan, I mean.'

His indifference delighted her. 'You are old, old friends, aren't you? Teresa says you are made for each other.'

'Don't believe all that Teresa tells you.' The alarm in Mark's voice heightened her delight. 'Your father is asleep,' Mark continued. He guided her to the side door. 'You can go in this way, back to your room. You should be in bed yourself.'

'I'm not going to bed,' demurred Ellen. 'I want to help you dress that awful man's wounded hand.' She sensed his hesitation. 'Please,' she begged. 'You have been so good to father and me. I want to be of some use, and that man may be difficult. I – I can hold your gun on him while you fix his bandage.'

Mark held the lantern to her face. The glow drew gold lights from her auburn hair.

There were dark smudges of weariness under her eyes, but the eyes were bright with eagerness.

'You win.' He continued to gaze at her. 'You are very beautiful,' he said, 'and wonderful.' He handed her the lantern and picked up the medical kit. 'Let's go.'

They made their way into the ranch yard, careful to avoid the little pools of water.

They reached the low adobe building that was the granary. Mark slid the bar and swung the door open, reminded himself not to forget to secure it with the padlock now in the office.

Ellen lifted the lantern. Its glow revealed the prisoner sitting on a pile of empty grain sacks. He looked like a sick man, gave them a pain-distorted grimace.

'I was thinkin' you figgered to leave me rot in this dump.'

'I'm taking a look at your hand,' Mark said. 'Not much we can do for it until the doctor comes.' He put the pan and box on the floor and picked up the cords he had left lying near the door.

'Let me have your gun,' Ellen said nervously. 'He looks so – so mean.'

Mark handed her the .45 from its holster. She stood there, tense, watchful, lantern in one hand, the gun in the other, while Mark tied the uninjured arm to the man's belt. He sponged the mangled hand with the disinfectant and adjusted a fresh bandage.

He removed the cords, retrieved the gun from Ellen and stood gazing thoughtfully at the sullen-faced prisoner. 'What's your name?' he asked.

'Ain't talkin'.'

'Who sent you to murder Mr Brice?'

'You done asked me them questions before. I told you I ain't talkin'.'

'Did Reeve Bett send you?'

The desperado's answer was an ugly grimace. Mark studied him with bleak eyes. 'You'll talk,' he said. 'You'll talk to save your own neck.'

'You ain't holdin' me long,' muttered the man. 'I got friends.'

Mark picked up the medical kit, motioned Ellen to step outside. He followed, swung the door shut and slid the bar. The blanket of the night again closed around them. Ellen repressed a shudder. 'That awful man,' she said. 'He frightens me.'

Mark seemed not to hear her, and she, too, now heard the vague stirrings that drifted through the stillness of the night. A long way off, a distant whispering of sound somewhere in that darkness.

'What is it?' Ellen wondered, fearfully.

'Riders,' Mark said. 'A lot of them.'

'Your men?'

Mark shook his head. 'They wouldn't be coming from town.' He took her arm. 'Let's get back to the house.'

Lucy Swan jumped up from the sofa when they entered the hall. Ignoring Ellen, she rushed to Mark.

'You've been so long,' she reproached him. 'I've been needing you so much.'

'Sorry, Lucy.' Mark deposited his pan and the box. 'I had some doctoring to do.'

Ellen handed him the lantern. 'Let me know if there's anything more I can do.' She disappeared into her bedroom.

Lucy Swan's gaze followed her thoughtfully. She was very pretty – too pretty – too friendly with Mark.

His voice broke into her jealous reflections. 'Lucy, when did it happen? Your father, I mean?'

'He was found in his hotel room this morning, shot dead.' She was tearful again, turned to the sofa. 'I didn't know what else to do, except come to you.'

'Ross Chaine would want to help. Have you sent word to him?'

'Ross isn't home. He's in Kansas City with a cattle shipment.' Lucy dabbed at her eyes. 'Anyway, it's *you* I want, not Ross.'

'He's crazy about you,' Mark said. 'He's going to be terribly upset – being away, and you needing help.'

'Ross is – is a dear, but he's not you,' Lucy told him tearfully. 'You're all the help I want.'

Mark sat down by her side, put an arm around her. 'What exactly happened to your father? Was it an accident?'

'Sheriff Corter said it was an accident, but Jim Stagg says it was murder.'

Mark's face hardened. Of the two opinions he was already accepting Jim Stagg's. The shrewd old liveryman must have good reasons for saying Bill Swan's death was murder. Mark thought of the sheriff's morning visit with Starkey and Reeve Bett, his too eager readiness to believe their accusations against Brice. Something was wrong there.

Lucy nestled close to him. 'Oh, Mark! I'm so frightened. I'm all alone now that father is dead.' Her head lifted in a surprised look at him as his arm dropped from her waist.

'Lucy–' He was on his feet now and she saw that he was listening intently. 'I've got to leave you. Somebody coming.'

Lucy sprang to her feet, her face pale. The sound was unmistakable. The dull thud of horses' hoofs. Mark drew his gun from its holster, examined it, thrust it back, motioned for her to stay where she was, and went swiftly to the hall door. It closed behind him.

Ellen had heard the approaching riders. She ran into the hall. Lucy swung on her high heels, looked at her.

'Mr Hudson is not needing your help this time,' she said. 'You mind your own business, Miss Brice.' No tears now. They were bright with hostility.

Ellen ignored the other girl's challenging manner. 'We heard them coming when we were in the yard. It might mean trouble for Mark.'

'It's the outfit returning from Willow Creek camp,' Lucy said. 'Teresa told me Mark was excepting them in any minute.'

Ellen shook her head. 'Mark doesn't think those riders are his outfit. He said they wouldn't be coming from town.' She suddenly ran into her father's room, reappeared in a few moments with a Colt .45 in her hand. She ran to the hall door. Lucy Swan, her mouth open, watched her disappear into the darkness outside.

CHAPTER SIX

The opening and closing of the door, the brief moment of hall light, apprised Mark he had been followed. He looked up from the veranda step, gun in lowered hand.

'Ellen!' He ran up the steps to where she stood. 'Ellen! Please go back!'

She said, coolly, 'If there's danger, I'm facing it with you.'

'Go back,' he pleaded. 'Please, Ellen—'

She gestured with her gun. 'They're coming—'

The riders emerged from the tree-lined avenue, spilled into the yard, vague shapes in the darkness. Mark gave the girl a frantic look.

'Go back,' he said again. 'Don't follow me.' He ran down the steps, was lost to view in the bushes near the garden gate.

Ellen hesitated, moved behind a veranda post where she could watch unseen by the newcomers in the yard. The horsemen halted close to the gate near where Mark crouched. A voice broke through the sudden hush, a voice that Mark evidently recognised. Ellen saw him emerge from the bushes and step to the gate.

'What do you want, Sheriff?' His voice was hard, unfriendly.

'Got bad news, Mark. There's been a killin' in town. Bill Swan.' The sheriff was climbing stiffly from his saddle. 'That gal of his, Lucy, is missing from the ranch and we're some worried.' He approached the gate Mark swung open, tall, gaunt, weary-visaged even in that darkness.

'Looks like she's been kidnapped, or something,' he rumbled.

'What's the posse for?' Mark holstered his gun.

'We're lookin' for the gal,' Corter said. 'We was out to the Swan ranch, figgerin' to pick up the killer's trail and found the gal was gone. Seen her mare layin' dead back there in the avenue.'

'Miss Swan is here, Sheriff,' Mark told him. 'She was on her way here to tell me about her father's death when her mare was hit by lightning.'

'You don't say,' ejaculated the sheriff. He looked over his shoulder at the cluster of silent riders. 'The gal is here, fellers.'

It was too dark for Mark to recognise any

of their faces. He said with forced hospitality: 'You could all do with some hot coffee after your long ride.'

'I'll say we can,' agreed the sheriff gratefully. 'Get down from your broncs, fellers.'

The riders drifted towards a corral fence, one of them leading the sheriff's horse. The diversion gave Ellen the chance to slip unnoticed into the hall. She was remembering that Mark did not want it known he was giving sanctuary to the Brice family.

'It's the sheriff and a posse,' she told Lucy, huddled disconsolately on the sofa. Teresa, hurrying from the kitchen, heard her. She threw up her hands despairingly.

'*Madre de Dios!* What next?'

'They want coffee.' Ellen paused. 'Mark does not want it known we are here, my father and I–' she threw Lucy Swan a warning look as she vanished into her bedroom, the Colt .45 clutched in her hand.

Teresa's gaze followed her. '*Madre de Dios!*' she repeated incredulously. 'She carries a gun!'

Lucy Swan, stiffly erect on the sofa, gave her an odd look. 'I don't like her. I want her out of here.'

There was a hint of doubt in the housekeeper's returning look. 'She is brave, that one... She was ready to fight.'

Lucy brushed impatiently at a dark curl. 'I don't care.' There was venom in her voice. 'I'm not keeping it a secret they're here in Mark's house. I've heard about them. Her father is a rustler. I'm betting the sheriff is here to get him.'

An unfortunate statement for Lucy to make to Teresa Cota who regarded Mark's wish as the law of the rancho. Her face reddened with anger.

'*Señorita*–' she spoke sternly. 'You will be very sorry if you betray our *Señor*. Watch your tongue, or you will answer to me who has always been your good friend.'

Lucy shrank back on the sofa. She had never seen Teresa so outraged, or heard her speak so fiercely. The housekeeper shook a finger at her as she turned towards the front door.

'Remember what I say,' she warned. 'Watch that jealous tongue.'

Mark and the sheriff were mounting the veranda steps. Teresa beamed at them from the doorway. 'Welcome, *Señor* Sheriff! You have come again for my coffee?'

'Coffee will sure hit the spot, Teresa,' chortled the sheriff. 'Quite a crowd of us this time.'

Teresa peered past him at the vague shapes in the dark ranch yard. 'How many?' she asked practically.

'Oh, maybe a dozen of us.'

'Is *Señor* Bett with you,' she wanted to know.

'You bet he ain't,' Sheriff Corter answered. 'Bett don't ride with a posse no time.' He gave the Mexican woman a shrewd look. 'What for you ask?'

'I don't like him,' Teresa told him frankly. 'I don't like snakes.' She flounced back in the hall. 'I'll tell Petra to get the coffee ready, and beef sandwiches.'

The sheriff followed Mark into the ranch office. 'She shouldn't talk thataways about Bett,' complained the lawman. 'Reeve Bett is the most important man we got. He stands ace-high with me.'

'Teresa and you wear different glasses,' Mark said. 'You two don't see Bett the same way.'

'Huh?' Sheriff Corter eased his lanky frame into a chair and fixed puzzled eyes on the younger man. 'I don't wear no glasses.'

'Forget it.' Mark swivelled his desk chair and dropped into it. 'Lucy Swan had just been telling me that you said the shooting was an accident. Now you tell me it was murder and that you and your posse were following the killer's trail to the Swan ranch, found Lucy was missing and picked up her tracks heading this way.'

Sheriff Corter reached inside a pocket for a plug of tobacco, slowly gnawed off a chew. It was plain he was flustered, searching his mind for a satisfactory explanation.

'It's like this, Mark. I wasn't there – didn't see the shootin'. Reeve Bett said Bill was foolin' with his gun, shot himself accidental, like I told the gal.'

'What made you change your mind?'

The sheriff replaced the plug of tobacco in his pocket, squirmed uncomfortably in his chair. 'Doc Brown found that Bill had been shot in the back, and that made it murder. Bill couldn't have shot himself in the back.'

'Jim Stagg told Lucy it was murder,' Mark said. 'I don't like it, Corter. I'm wondering why Reeve Bett told you it was an accident, and why you took his word for it.'

'I ain't likin' your questions much,' complained the lawman. 'I only know that some fellers told Reeve it was an accident.'

Mark studied him thoughtfully. 'Lucy says Bill was found dead this morning in his room at the hotel where he had spent the night.'

'That's right. I didn't hear about it until I got back to town with Starkey and Bett after our talk with you.' He sighed wearily. 'One hell of a day. Me and Jim took him back to the ranch and broke the news to Lucy. Was caught in the storm before we made it back to town.'

'You must have known about the shot in the back,' Mark said. 'Jim Stagg knew ... told Lucy it was murder.'

The sheriff's face reddened. 'I figgered the doc was wrong and that Reeve was right. I wasn't telling Reeve he was a liar.'

'It's a queer, mixed-up affair.' Mark's tone was curt. 'I don't like it. You're the sheriff, not Reeve Bett. What are you afraid of?'

'Sure I'm the sheriff,' fumed Corter. 'I ain't afraid of him, nor of you.' His big hands clenched the arms of his chair. 'I ain't takin' that talk from you.'

Mark ignored the bluster. 'You said you had a clue that led to the Swan ranch.'

'The trail kind of petered out,' Corter confessed. 'All we know is the killer's a stranger ... seen ridin' a bronc wearing the Swan brand.'

Mark was silent. It was in his mind the sheriff was lying. The thought troubled him. There was only one answer. Reeve Bett had

71

the sheriff in his pocket.

Teresa came into the room with a tray loaded with coffee and sandwiches. Sheriff Corter's face brightened. He rid himself of the tobacco-cud and reached eagerly for a cup.

'Looking after the boys?' he asked.

'*Si*–' Teresa beamed. 'They're in the kitchen.' She looked at Mark. '*Señorita* Swan has gone back to her room. She will see you later, she says.'

Mark nodded. 'Tell her I won't be long.'

The housekeeper gave the sheriff a parting smile as she left them. His eager attention to the beef sandwiches gratified her.

One member of the posse was not in the kitchen. Something in the ranch yard had intrigued him. Alone now, he studied certain imprints in the mud. He peered at them intently in the darkness. Footprints that led from the Brice ranch-wagon to the adobe granary. There were other tracks in the mud, leading from the garden gate. He gazed at the barred door. No padlock. He glanced cautiously at the garden gate. Only the rumble of men's voices from the kitchen, his fellow-members of the posse enjoying coffee and sandwiches.

Satisfied there was no one to see, he slid

the bar, opened the door and peered at the man sitting on the pile of sacks.

'Cherokee,' he whispered. 'What the hell–' He slipped inside, helped Mark's prisoner to his feet.

'Quick, Slade,' Cherokee muttered. 'Get me out of here fast. That Hudson hombre's a devil on wheels.' His curiosity mounted. 'What you fellers doin' here? Heard you ride into the yard.'

'Old Corter's huntin' sign for a killer,' grinned Slade, a tall, swarthy man. 'The boss fixed it for me to ride with the posse.'

'They found old Swan, huh?'

'They sure did.' Slade swore softly. 'Shootin' him in the back was one fool play ... put the doc wise it wan't no accident.'

'Wasn't nothin' else I could do.' Cherokee scowled. 'Swan seen me come in the room ... was goin' for his gun fast.'

He followed Slade through the door. Slade closed it, slid the bar into its slot. He looked nervously off at the garden gate. 'I've got to get over there with the other fellers. Don't want 'em to know about me turnin' you loose. Where's your bronc?'

'In the barn, I reckon, and feller, I'm sure cravin' to fork saddle.' Cherokee stared down at his bandage. 'Cain't throw on my saddle easy with this busted hand. You got to help me.' He started at a shuffling run towards the barn.

Slade reluctantly followed. 'How did you get your hand smashed?' he asked.

'Hudson's bullet.' Cherokee spat an oath. 'My fault for not gettin' him this morning when he was standin' back there on the porch.'

They slipped inside the barn, closed the door, stood for a few moments, accustoming their eyes to the pitch darkness. Cherokee muttered an exclamation. 'Looks like my pinto in this first stall ... saddle still on him.' In another minute he led the horse from the stall. 'Make sure the cinch is tight, Slade.'

Slade took a pull at the girth. Cherokee climbed awkwardly into the saddle. His fellow-renegade opened the door, took a cautious look outside, motioned to Cherokee that all was clear.

Out in the yard again, Slade closed the stable door. When he turned, Cherokee was already spurring the pinto across the yard. Slade scowled at the rider fading into the darkness. There were things he wanted to ask Cherokee. He would liked to have learned how Cherokee happened to be a prisoner in the granary. Cherokee had been mighty scared and awfully anxious to put distance between himself and the Hudson ranch.

Slade hurried his step. The boys would be wondering what was keeping him.

CHAPTER SEVEN

Reeve Bett stood in the doorway of his office, thoughtfully contemplating the two-storey frame building on the opposite corner of the street. A man was putting a coat of white paint on its weather-stained walls. A second man was finishing a sign that hung from the balcony above the veranda steps. The large black letters on the white background spelled the words, SAN CARLOS HOTEL.

Satisfaction was in his fox-bright eyes as he watched. He had done well since his arrival in the town. Now that Bill Swan was out of the way he was the undisputed owner of the hotel, another gold mine to add to his profitable Roundup Saloon. He thought of the deeds and mortgages and gold accumulating in the steel box under a floor-board in his office. It was, he decided, about time to expand his present office into a bank. The town needed a bank.

He gazed up and down the muddy street along which the late evening shadows were fast crawling. A drab scene, typical of any little town of the border west. Only a couple of horses drooping at the long hitch-rail in front of the Roundup Saloon. Too early for the usual influx of riders from the outlying ranches. Kramer's General Merchandise Store was the only other place still open for business. Sol Kramer, a stout, red-faced man with a head of bushy grey hair, was helping a belated storm-bound rancher load a plough into his wagon.

Reeve Bett's eyes narrowed as he watched. The store was another little gold mine. He would have to do some thinking about Kramer. There were ways of making the stout storekeeper decide that San Carlos was an unhealthy place – be more willing to turn his prosperous business over to a smarter man.

Bett turned back to his office, pushed through the door and sank into his desk chair. The night was closing in fast. He got up, lit the lamp on the desk, stood for a few moments, gazing at the fading twilight beyond the window. It was time Corter and the posse were back in town from the wild goose chase on which he had sent them. The sheriff would have soon learned that the man seen riding from town on a Swan horse was only a member of the Swan outfit and had nothing to do with the murder. Too bad Cherokee had messed the thing up, given Doc Brown cause to say Bill Swan's death was murder and not the accident he had wanted officially pronounced.

Bett drew a cigar from his gold case, lit it and leaned back in his chair. He felt suddenly depressed, aware of uneasy misgivings. The day had developed some disquieting facts. The accident he had planned for Swan had officially become murder. Swan's own fault that he had to die. His stubborn insistence that Saval's bill-of-sale for the hotel was a forgery was his death warrant. Swan and Saval had been old friends, and Swan claimed that Saval was unable to write his signature because of a paralysed hand.

Bett scowled as he recalled that last conversation with Bill Swan the evening before the murder. He had not known that Swan was the executor of Saval's estate. The fraudulent bill-of-sale seemed easy enough to get away with.

'I'm taking it up with the law,' Swan told him as he left the office. 'Hank Saval gave me his power-of-attorney because he couldn't write his name, and I never signed that bill-of-sale you're claiming makes you the owner of his San Carlos hotel.'

It was then that Bett had instructed Cherokee to follow Bill Swan to his hotel room where he was staying the night.

Bett's teeth savagely maltreated his cigar. Cherokee had blundered, made murder of what was to have been an accident caused by Swan's carelessness with his own gun. He had blundered again, failed to get Mark Hudson, later that morning. He fervently hoped his hired killer had not failed on his mission to the Brice ranch.

Hudson and Brice! Two men dangerous to his ambitions, more danger than perhaps they knew. Hudson, respected by all who knew him for his integrity and fearlessness. He was shrewd, able to add two and two and get the correct answer, an answer that would tear the mask from the man responsible for the growing depredations of the cattle rustlers, the reign of terror that was already causing the smaller ranchers to shake the dust of San Carlos from their feet.

It was also possible that Brice had told Hudson the real purpose that had brought him to the San Carlos in the role of a homesteader. Hudson was doubly the menace to be eliminated, and soon.

It had been a shock when Brice had settled on his little ranch on the border. The man was a deadly peril to his plans, in fact to his freedom. He had not known Brice was in the country until the time he had ridden out there to make an offer to buy him out. He only knew that some new-comers were living in dangerous proximity to the maze of canyons the rustlers found useful for holding stolen cattle.

The cigar in Bett's fingers trembled as he recalled those horrifying moments when he rode into the yard and realised the new-comer was Samuel Brice, the former Boston banker whom he had ruined and brought to shame. To his vast relief, Brice had failed to recognise Pollett Quin in Reeve Bett. The Pollett Quin, Brice had reason to remem-ber, was a yellow-haired, smooth-faced man. Reeve Bett's hair, the neat beard and moustache he now cultivated, had the black sheen of a crow's wing, thanks to careful and continual dyeing.

Bett produced a flask from a desk drawer and tipped it to his lips. The swallow drew a shudder from him. He seldom drank, pre-ferred to leave liquor to the fools who nightly thronged the Roundup Saloon, to his profit.

He returned the bottle to the drawer and looked at his watch. About time he went over to the hotel for his dinner. He'd wait a little longer for the sheriff to get back from the Swan ranch. He was curious to know how the Swan girl was taking the death of her father. A good-looker, Lucy Swan, and she was now the sole owner of the Swan ranch.

Bett allowed his imagination to trifle a few minutes with Lucy. She would make a proper wife for a man like himself. Her father's spoiled darling, a soft, pretty exterior, and yet he sensed a hardness in her, a self-seeking nature that could be useful to him. He made a mental note to drive over to the Swan ranch the next day with his condolences, offer his protection against the cattle rustlers.

Bett's moustache lifted in a cynical smile. Yes, he would see to it that Lucy's cattle were not stolen. Their safety though, would depend on how she received his attentions.

He stared thoughtfully at the glowing tip of his cigar. The Brice girl was a good-looker, too. Brice had not liked his apparent interest in his daughter. The old man had bristled like a wolf.

Bett's moustache twitched in another little smile. The old man needn't worry. The Brice girl was a dead issue now Lucy Swan was on the scene, as dead as her father was by this time if Cherokee had accomplished his murderous mission. Too bad for Cherokee if he had again missed his target...

The half-breed was doing some hard thinking for himself as he fled from the Hudson ranch yard. His last two attempts at murder had gone wrong. Dull of wit as he was, Cherokee instinctively knew that Reeve Bett had no use for a man who failed him. The road back to town would lead to his own sudden death.

Cherokee swung his horse from the road into a trail that wound through the chaparral towards the Mexican border. He was not sure his strength would hold out for the ride to safety below the border. Something was wrong with him. His bullet-smashed hand throbbed with agonising pain that left him dizzy. He pushed doggedly on, spurs raking the weary horse. Anything was better than facing Reeve Bett.

Unaware of his hired killer's flight, Bett stubbed his cigar in an ashtray and got out of his chair. No use waiting for Sheriff Corter. He was wanting his dinner. He turned the lamp down, blew out the light, closed and locked his door and crossed the street to the hotel, pausing to admire the fresh white coat of paint – the new sign that swung above the balcony steps. *His* hotel, now.

Engrossed with his pleasing thoughts, Bett

failed to notice the vague shape watching him from the darker area between his office and the saloon. He mounted the steps and disappeared inside the hotel lobby.

Fidel cautiously emerged from the alley, and careful to avoid the revealing light of the swing-lamp over the saloon, he turned up the street towards the Stagg Livery and Feed Stables, restraining the impulse to run. Undue haste might draw unwelcome attention.

Hardly an hour had passed since his arrival at the *cantina* of his uncle, Juan Moraga, in Old Town. He should have been in by mid-afternoon. The storm had caught him after leaving the Willow Creek camp and the cloudburst had forced him to make several long detours. Pat Race had warned him not to attempt the trip.

'You won't make it, kid,' the Bar H foreman said. 'The trails will be washed to hell and gone when the storm hits. She's going to hit awful soon and hard. I'm not sendin' Tulsa back to the ranch until she's blown over. Tulsa's too old to go fightin' cloudbursts.'

Fidel chose to disregard the foreman's warning. His boss had given him a job to do and he was going to do it even at the risk of his own life. He wasn't old, like Tulsa.

'You're a young fool,' Pat Race told him. 'Be your own fault if you're drowned.'

Fidel was close to being drowned more than once. He reached his uncle's *cantina*, weary and mud-splattered, his horse exhausted. Dry clothes were found for him, and hot drink and food. The resilience of youth quickly overcame fatigue and he was soon eager to be on his way to Jim Stagg with his boss's note. Before he could leave the *cantina* he was to share the amazement of his Uncle Juan at the appearance of his great-grandfather, Fernando Cota. They could hardly believe their eyes.

Their surprise amused the aged ex-vaquero. 'I am not a ghost.' He swaggered to a chair. 'Quick, Juan – a drink!' Despite his bravado, his weariness was apparent. His hand lifted in a gesture. 'Juan – take a message to the doctor. He is needed at the rancho. I do not know where he lives, so you must go for me.'

'I will go,' readily assented the owner of the *cantina*. He gazed at his great-grandfather, horrified.

'Our *Señor!* He is hurt?' He formed the question with stiff lips.

'No, no – not the *Señor.*' Fernando's voice rumbled on as he sipped the wine Juan

Moraga hastily served him. He told them the happenings at the ranch. 'No one there to come for the doctor, so I, Fernando Cota, ride again for the rancho as always when danger threatens...' He shook his head worriedly. 'Almost I ran into the sheriff and his posse on their way to the rancho. I hid in the brush, did not let them see me. Something is very wrong. I don't like it.'

'I go for the doctor,' Juan Moraga said. He hurried from the room.

Fidel came out of his shock. He turned to the door. 'I have business,' he said. 'I will see you later.' He disappeared into the night.

The sight of Reeve Bett appearing from his office, held him in the dark alley. His boss had sent him to town to keep eyes and ears open. Anything he learned about Bett was important.

A freight outfit was pulling into the big livery yard, bells jingling on the lead mules. Tall, gaunt-framed Jim Stagg stood under the glare of the kerosene lamp that swung above the entrance, watching the mule-skinner swing his great wagons around the turn. He gave the young Mexican a sharp look of recognition, held out a hand for the note Fidel thrust at him, motioned at the office doorway.

'Be with you in a minute,' he said. 'I've got to see Jack about when he wants his mules to have their grain. He's mighty cranky about them mules.'

The minutes dragged. Fidel relaxed.

'Well, son–'

Jim Stagg's voice from the doorway jerked Fidel to his feet.

'Catchin' some shut-eye, huh?' The livery-man settled into his chair, boot heels on desk. 'You look some tired, young feller.'

'*Es nada.*' Fidel resumed his seat on the bench. 'The storm made the trails bad or I would have been here hours ago with the note from my boss. I stopped in Old Town for dry clothes,' he added.

'Lucky you got here safe,' Jim Stagg said. His keen eyes appraised the young Mexican thoughtfully. 'I've read Mark Hudson's note. He says you're in town to use your eyes and ears for him.'

'*Si, Señor–*'

Stagg extracted the note from a pocket, studied it, a hint of worry in his eyes. 'He says a feller wearing a red calfskin vest and ridin' a pinto bronc, took a shot at him this morning. He figgers that maybe Reeve Bett is mixed up in it.'

'He is a bad man,' Fidel said.

'He's a dangerous man.' Stagg crumpled the note and dropped it in a waste basket. 'You're some young to be lockin' horns with him?'

'I am a man, *Señor.*' Fidel's chin lifted proudly.

The old liveryman nodded approval. 'I reckon you are, or Mark wouldn't be sending you on a job like this.' His eyes narrowed thoughtfully. 'This red calfskin vest feller could be a feller they call Cherokee,' he mused. 'Rides a pinto and is sure one pizen snake. Ain't been in town long.'

'I kill snakes,' Fidel said.

'Pizen snakes like Cherokee don't warn you like a rattler does,' Stagg told him grimly. He was silent for a moment. 'All right, Fidel. We'll let folks think you're working for me at the barn. Like Mark says, you can pick up news that don't reach *my* ears.'

'I have news for you,' Fidel said. He told the interested liveryman about Fernando's arrival in Old Town in quest of a doctor – the old vaquero's account of the happenings at the ranch.

'I never expected to see that old-timer fork a saddle ag'in,' marvelled the liveryman. Worry deepened the lines on his craggy face. 'Only plenty trouble would be getting old Fernando out of his arm chair.'

'The man who shot Brice is now a prisoner in the granary,' Fidel told him.

'My great-grandfather did not say the man's name – only that he was wounded when my boss took him prisoner.'

'I ain't liking it.' Stagg's boot heels gouged fresh scars on his desk. 'Somebody is mighty anxious to get Mark and old Brice, the way they got Bill Swan this morning.'

'My great-grandfather also said he saw the sheriff and his posse riding to the ranch. He hid in the brush for fear they would see him. He was worried.' Fidel hesitated, added cautiously, 'There is talk that Brice is a cow thief.'

Stagg slid his booted feet from the desk with a bang that shook the floor. 'Brice ain't no cow thief, young feller.' Anger reddened his face. 'He's my friend, and Mark's friend. We don't side with rustlers no time.'

Alone in his office, Jim Stagg leaned wearily back in his chair. He was thinking that sunrise must see him on his way to the Hudson ranch. Mark was in trouble, and Mark was his friend.

CHAPTER EIGHT

Dr Brown finished adjusting the bandage and picked up the flattened piece of lead extracted from his patient's shoulder. He scowled at it. 'Nasty thing–' He tossed the bullet to Mark.

'You're a lucky man, Mr Brice.' A smile brightened the doctor's lean, weary face. 'A little more to the left and the bullet would have found your heart.' He busied himself for a few moments with his stethoscope. 'Shock and exposure haven't done you any good, but a few days will put you on your feet again.'

He closed his bag, looked at Mark. 'Where's this other man you say needs me?'

'I'll take you to him.' Mark was looking at Brice, a hint of worry in his eyes. The concern in the doctor's face when using the stethoscope had not escaped him. 'Is there anything more you'll want to do for Mr Brice?'

'Rest, rest, plenty of rest,' Dr Brown said. 'That's all I can prescribe for him. I'll be out again in a day or two.'

A timid knock on the door swung them from the bedside. It opened and Ellen peered in at them, a hand hugging a blue robe over her nightdress.

'How is he?' she asked in a whisper. 'I can't sleep unless I know he's all right.'

'I'm fine, Ellen,' Brice said from the pillow. 'You go back to your bed.'

Mark quietly closed the door as Ellen joined him in the hall, and for a moment they stood gazing at each other. Suddenly she was in his arms, lips on his.

They drew apart, breathless, shaken. Mark said, a bit unsteadily, 'I couldn't help it. You're so wonderful.'

Ellen pulled her robe over a bare shoulder. Her eyes were starry, even in that dim hall light. 'I – I don't want you to help it – ever.' She fled into her bedroom.

Teresa and the doctor reappeared in the hall. The doctor looked annoyed. 'The girl wants you to take her back to the ranch to-night,' he told Mark. 'You can't do it ... you're dead on your feet right now.' There was frank disapproval in Dr Brown's voice. 'I'm dreadfully sorry for Lucy, but she's letting grief make her selfish, think of only herself.'

'The doctor is right,' Teresa said firmly. 'You must rest, Markito. You are not made of iron, as I have just told *Señorita* Swan.'

Mark hardly heard her. The feel of Ellen in his arms still lingered with him. He said, almost curtly, 'We need a lantern from the kitchen.'

'Delfina will bring you one.' Teresa hurried away, a disturbed look in her eyes.

Waiting in the hall for the lantern, Mark said hesitantly, 'I was watching you go over Brice with your stethoscope. You weren't pleased.'

'You've guessed right. Bad heart ... that's why I insisted upon rest.'

'That's tough on him,' Mark said gloomily. 'He has troubles enough.'

'People can live for years with a bad heart,' the doctor said. 'Brice can, too, if he's careful.'

'It's hard to be careful when murder is on your trail,' Mark said unhappily.

Dr Brown nodded. 'There's a lot of devilry going on, Mark. We've got to do something about it.' He shook his grey-maned head. 'Poor Bill Swan, as fine as they come. It was cold-blooded murder, and nobody seems to know how it happened, least of all our fool of a sheriff.'

Delfina appeared with the lantern. Mark took it from her and led the way down the veranda steps. Stars blazed overhead as they crossed the yard to the granary, the lantern light dancing on the pools of water. As his hand went to the draw-bar Mark again reminded himself to get the padlock from the office. He hadn't thought to bring it with him.

He slid the bar and opened the door, muttered a startled exclamation, stood there, dismayed, the lantern in uplifted hand.

'Nobody here,' Dr Brown said.

'He's gone ... escaped!' Mark's incredulous gaze swept the granary. 'Somebody helped him get away.'

He swung the heavy door shut, slid the bar back into place, stared at it with bleak eyes. The man could not possibly have opened the door from the inside. Somebody had opened it for him. There was only one answer. The sheriff's posse.

Boot tracks in the mud led to the barn. Mark and the doctor followed them. A brief look inside the stable told Mark the wounded desperado's pinto horse was missing.

Mark closed the stable door, furious with himself. His own fault the prisoner had escaped. He should have attended to the pad-lock.

Dr Brown sensed the worry gnawing him. 'Is it serious, the man getting away?' he asked.

'I didn't want it known Brice is here,' Mark told him. 'No chance to keep it a secret, now the man is on the loose again. He'll tell the scoundrel who hired him to murder Brice – and me.'

'You can depend on me to keep it a secret about Brice,' the doctor assured him.

'I'm not worried about you, Doc.'

'You didn't tell me there's been an attempt on your life, too,' reproached Dr Brown.

'The same man took a shot at me this morning.'

'It's fiendish,' muttered the doctor. 'Poor Bill Swan already dead, and now you and Brice marked for murder.'

He rubbed his chin reflectively. 'Have you any idea who's responsible for this – this dastardly plot?'

'I can make a guess.'

'I'm your friend, Mark. I'd like to know whom you suspect.'

'Reeve Bett,' Mark said. 'No proof – yet.'

'Impossible!' Dr Brown frowned. 'Not Bett? He's one of our leading citizens.'

'A lot of border riff-raff has moved into San Carlos since he came to town,' Mark said.

'That's a fact,' agreed the doctor. 'A sorry fact. It hadn't occurred to me that Bett was responsible.'

'There have been other unexplained killings,' Mark reminded him. 'Small ranchers – homesteaders who have mysteriously disappeared, or been frightened away.'

'That's right,' agreed Dr Brown, his kindly, lean face grim in the glow of the lantern in Mark's hand. 'I've been too busy to notice these things, but come to think of it, Reeve's growing prosperity makes me wonder.' The doctor paused, added reflectively, 'Why, only this morning I learned that he has acquired full ownership of Hank Saval's hotel. In fact he showed me the deed Saval signed shortly before his death.'

Mark stiffened. 'That's odd,' he said. 'Saval had a paralysed arm. He couldn't write his signature.'

'I should know he couldn't. I was his doctor.'

'Bill Swan had Saval's power-of-attorney,' Mark continued. 'If Bill's signature is not on that deed, the thing is a forgery.'

'Heaven help us?' muttered the doctor.

'Bill's signature was not on the deed Bett showed me this morning.' He looked at Mark, his face grey and haggard in the lantern's light. 'And Bill was murdered this morning!'

'Yes,' Mark said quietly. 'Bill Swan is dead, unable to prove the deed is a forgery.'

The two men walked in silence across the yard to the doctor's buggy. Mark unfastened the team's tie-rope while his friend climbed in and picked up the reins.

'You should have a cup of coffee before starting back to town,' he said.

Dr Brown shook his head regretfully. 'I'm overdue in town now. Sol Kramer's wife is expecting a baby any time tonight. I've got to be there.'

Mark stood for a long moment by the hitch-rail, gaze following the mud-splattered buggy swing out of the yard and fade into the darkness. His thoughts were in a turmoil of futile conjectures about the prisoner's escape from the granary. He had hoped to force a confession from the man, obtain proof that Reeve Bett was the instigator of the murderous attacks, evidence that would unmask him as the leader of the ruthless gang terrorising the San Carlos Country.

Teresa Cota was watching for him from the

veranda steps. She peered at him, wonder in her eyes.

'You look like the Old *Señor*,' she marvelled. 'The same fighting look that was his when danger stalked the rancho.'

Mark was not listening. He halted, a foot on the step, gazed back into the darkness beyond the gate.

Teresa said, fright in her hushed voice, 'Riders coming!'

A well-known voice faintly reached them above the dull thud of hoofs in the rain-softened road. The tenseness went from Mark.

'Pat Race!' he exclaimed, vast relief in the smile he gave the housekeeper.

'Thanks be to the saints!' Teresa touched the little silver cross on her bosom. 'I will tell Petra to start the coffee-pot and heat the beef stew. Those vaqueros have the appetites of wolves.'

Mark hurried into the yard, his weariness forgotten. His experienced ears told him that some half-dozen riders of the Bar H outfit accompanied the foreman. He waited near the long water-trough, watched them emerge from the avenue, vague shapes in the blanketing night.

Pat Race was the first to pull up at the

water-trough. Mark had only a glance for him. His attention was fixed on a horse one of the riders had on a lead-rope. A black and white pinto he had reason to remember. Lashed to the saddle was the wounded desperado his carelessness had allowed to escape from the granary.

The Bar H foreman saw his amazement. 'We ran into the feller up the trail aways,' he said. 'He was layin' there, groaning and kinder out of his head. Nothing to do but fetch him along with us...' Pat Race slid from his saddle, led his horse to the trough. 'You act like you seen him before,' he added.

'Yes, I've seen him before,' Mark said. 'I'm glad to see him again, Pat.'

'Looks like he's been in a gun-fight,' the foreman said. 'He's sure goin' to lose that arm unless we get him to a doc awful quick. Blood poisoning, I reckon.'

The other riders were lining their horses at the trough, among them, Tulsa, a leather-visaged, bow-legged little man who gave Mark an apologetic grin.

'Mighty sorry I couldn't get here sooner, Boss,' he said.

'I wasn't lettin' Tulsa buck that cloud-burst,' hastily interposed the foreman. 'It sure was one grandaddy of a storm, Mark.

97

The dry spell is busted for keeps.'

Two of the men were lifting Cherokee from his saddle. Mark motioned at the granary. 'In there,' he said.

Pat Race looked at him curiously. 'What for you throwing him in the granary?' he asked.

Mark's gaze followed his prisoner stumbling across the yard, supported by the two cowboys. The man's condition was serious. He would have to do something about it.

'He's awful sick,' the foreman said. 'Say the word and I'll send Brasca to town for the doc.'

'No chance to get Dr Brown out here tonight again,' Mark told him. 'He's busy with a childbirth – Sol Kramer's wife.'

'Why was Doc Brown here?' The tall foreman stood straggle-legged, fingers shaping a cigarette. 'Is old Fernando dyin'?'

'It's Brice,' Mark explained. 'That man you picked up on the trail shot him this morning, took a shot at me. I've got Brice and his daughter in the house now. Somebody wants to run Brice off his ranch ... murder him – murder me.'

'I'll be damned!' Pat Race stared at him. 'A killer, huh?' The foreman's voice took on a rasp. 'Hell, he don't need a doc. A rope on his neck is the medicine for him, and quick about it.'

'Not yet,' Mark said. 'He's too valuable, our big chance to get a line on the man who hired his gun. We've got to keep him alive, Pat, at least long enough to make him talk.'

'I savvy–' A match flared against the foreman's thumbnail. He touched the flame to his cigarette. 'It ties up with this rustlin' that's going on.'

'That's right. Somebody with brains back of it.' Mark looked questioningly at the foreman who tossed the cigarette down, heeled it into the soft, wet earth. He knew the signs. Pat had news he was reluctant to divulge.

'A tough day,' the foreman said. 'Tough for all of us.'

'I wasn't expecting you in from the camp.' Mark was sure of it now. Pat had bad news. 'I'm glad you got here. Nobody around to help ... Fidel in town and only old Fernando to send for the doctor.'

'Fernando!' ejaculated the foreman. 'Are you telling me he's forkin' saddle ag'in.'

'You should have seen him,' Mark said, fond pride in his voice. 'Champing at the bit like a two-year old.'

Pat Race nodded, his face solemn. 'Fernando sure goes on the prod when trouble hits the ranch.' He paused, looked down at the mangled cigarette. 'I hate to tell you, Mark. Willow Creek is short some two hundred head of cows. We've combed every place for 'em.' The foreman gestured angrily. 'They just ain't there.'

'Rustlers,' Mark said.

'Ain't no other answer,' growled Pat. 'I didn't think they'd have the nerve to rustle Bar H.'

The two men looked at each other. Mark said grimly, 'I told you somebody with brains is running the show, but it's possible he can be a fool, too.'

The cowboys who had taken Cherokee to the granary joined their companions emerging from the stable.

'Teresa is ready for you in the kitchen,' Mark told them as they trooped up.

'We're sure headin' there pronto, just as quick as we wash up some,' chuckled Brasca. 'Me – I'm hungry enough to chaw bob wire.'

Mark watched as they crowded through the garden gate. Vast relief surged through him. The presence of these tough, vigilant men meant added safety for Ellen.

Pat Race was speaking. 'I left Rusty Hall in charge of the camp. If you say the word I'll send for him and the rest of the boys to come, bring Old Sinful with 'em to cook. Teresa won't want Petra to cook for the outfit while we're here.' His boot heel dug again at the mangled cigarette. 'I figger you'll want us stickin' close for awhile, Mark.'

'That's right.' Mark nodded. 'Anything can happen.' He considered for a moment. 'I'll let you know in the morning.'

'What about the feller in the granary?' asked Pat. 'He's in bad shape.'

'It's up to you and me,' Mark said. 'It won't be the first time we've doctored a shot-up man on this ranch.'

'I reckon we can fix him up proper.' The foreman's smile was wintry. 'Save him for the hangman, after he's told us what you want to know about his boss.'

CHAPTER NINE

Jim Stagg sat in his buckboard under the cottonwood tree that shaded the hitch-rail in the Swan ranch yard. A score or more ranchers and their women were slowly filtering into the yard from the garden where they had just witnessed the slain rancher's interment. They gathered in small groups near their respective buggies and ranch wagons, their faces sober, voices hushed as they discussed the tragedy that had left Lucy Swan an orphan.

Ed Starkey and Reeve Bett were among the subdued throng. They gave the liveryman nods of recognition as they climbed into Bett's flashy red-wheeled buggy alongside his own buckboard.

'Sad affair,' Bett said. 'My heart bleeds for that poor girl.' He picked up the reins. 'Well, such is life.'

Jim Stagg's gaze followed them morosely as the red-wheeled buggy sped out of the yard. 'The damn hypocrite,' he muttered. 'Stones don't bleed.'

The groups were slowly disintegrating. Buggies and wagons rattled from the yard, a few riders from the more distant ranches. Jim Stagg continued to wait. He wanted to see Mark Hudson whose buckskin horse was still tied to the hitch-rail.

The sun blazed from a molten sky; despite the deep shade of the cottonwood tree, the liveryman was uncomfortably warm under his unaccustomed black coat. He peeled it off, threw it on the back seat. The heat was making him drowsy. Footsteps, the rasp of spurs, jerked him upright. His brief hope faded. The man approaching the hitch-rail was not Mark.

Stagg watched sleepily while the newcomer untied the horse next to Mark's buckskin. Not a Swan rider ... the brand on the horse was not the Swan iron. Probably a man hired to dig the grave. He seemed to have come from the garden gate. Something familiar about him.

Recognition dawned as the man slid into his saddle and rode away. He'd seen him before, hanging around the saloon in town, a hard-looking character who had recently drifted in from the border. *Slade* that was the name.

The liveryman was aware of a growing uneasiness. He could think of no reason why the man should attend Bill Swan's funeral. He was a stranger, and certainly no friend of Bill's; and as for the grave, the men of the Swan outfit would have seen to that sad task.

Jim Stagg drew a large handkerchief from his pocket and wiped his moist brow. He wanted more than ever now to see Mark, tell him about the curious incident. What could be keeping Mark so long back in the house anyway?

At that moment Mark was gently freeing himself from Lucy's arms.

'I've got to go,' he said.

'Please stay,' she begged. 'I need you, Mark.' She gestured tragically. 'I'm feeling so alone in the world – now that Dad is gone.'

'Mrs Saunders is here–'

Lucy smoothed her black dress over shapely hips. 'You're mean to me,' she tearfully reproached. 'You wouldn't even bring me home last night.'

'I couldn't get away and the best I could do was to have Pat Race drive you home. You insisted upon going.'

'I wasn't going to sleep under the same roof with that girl – her father a cow thief.'

Mark's silence was added fuel to her jealousy.

'You're dying to get back to her!' she furiously accused him. 'That's why you're in such a hurry to leave.'

'I've business in town,' Mark said. 'Don't talk nonsense, Lucy.' He reached for his hat.

'I'm not fooled,' she flared. 'You wouldn't drive me home last night because you didn't want to leave her, and now you want to get back to her as fast as you can.' She sank into a chair. 'Leave me for her,' she sobbed, 'and my poor father just in his grave.'

Mark gazed about the room distractedly. He was getting a surprising picture of Lucy Swan and not enjoying it. He could find no words for her, turned to the door.

Lucy sprang to her feet. 'I hate you – I hate you!'

The door closed behind him.

Jim Stagg loosed the reins from the whip-socket as Mark approached from the patio gate. 'Well,' he drawled, 'I reckon we're the last of the mourners, Mark.'

Mark snatched the buckskin's tie-rope loose, turned a worried look on the livery-man. 'Lucy is taking it hard,' he said.

'Sure she is.' Stagg wagged his head sadly. 'Mighty tough on her, losing a pa like Bill Swan. One of the best, Bill was.'

'She's not much like him,' Mark said a bit

grimly, and then silently reproached himself. There had been some truth in Lucy's accusations. He *had* wanted to be near Ellen the night before, and he *was* eager to get back to her again... Her safety was his greatest concern.

Stagg's voice broke into his thoughts. 'I was waiting for you, Mark ... want to talk things over with you – Fidel Cota for instance.'

'I'm heading for town,' Mark told him.

'Fine! Hitch your buck horse to the rig and set with me. We can talk drivin' in.'

'There's a lot you don't know we can talk about,' Mark said, busy with the buckskin's tie-rope. He climbed into the seat. 'What's on your mind, Jim?'

'There was a feller here, a few minutes before you come–' The buckboard careened in a sharp turn as Stagg flicked the backs of the team with his whip. In a moment they were whirling across the yard towards the gate, Mark's buckskin trailing at the gallop. The liveryman gave Mark a sheepish grin. 'I wasn't thinkin' or I wouldn't have laid the whip on 'em. They can't abide the whip. Come close to spillin' us – the dang fools.' He pushed the whip back in its socket. 'Well – this feller showed from nowhere, maybe the garden or the barn. I was kind of drowsin' ... didn't see him until he was at the hitch-rail untying his bronc. Wasn't a Swan man ... I know 'em all, and the bronc wasn't wearin' the Swan brand. It wasn't until he rode off that I remembered seeing him in town, a feller name of Slade ... hangs around with the tough saloon crowd.'

Mark shook his head. 'I don't know him.'

'I couldn't figger what he was doing here at Bill's funeral,' continued Stagg. 'I recognised his bronc, too, a red roan that Ed Starkey sold to Reeve Bett.'

'You interest me,' Mark said, his tone thoughtful.

'I figgered you'd be interested.' Stagg started to reach for the buggy whip, withdrew his hand with an annoyed grunt. 'Fidel Cota was telling me him and you got ideas about Reeve Bett.'

'That's right, and you have too, Jim.'

'The feller's a smooth-talkin' crook,' exploded Stagg. 'He's got Ed Starkey and the sheriff eatin' out of his hand. I ain't liking it, Mark, and I ain't liking this mystery about Bill Swan's murder.'

'A lot of queer things have been happening,' Mark said. 'I'm going to find out who's responsible. I've reason to believe Reeve Bett suspects my intentions.' He told the interested liveryman about the warning Brice had found on his barn door, and Cherokee's two attempts at murder. The Brice affair was news to Stagg.

'Fidel told me some feller had taken a shot at you, but he didn't say nothin' about Brice.'

'Fidel doesn't know about it,' Mark said. 'Nobody knows about Brice, or that I'm hiding him at Bar H. Only Doctor Brown and he promised to keep it a secret.'

'It's mighty lucky Pat Race run across the half-breed,' Stagg said. 'He'd have spilled the news to his boss if he'd got into town.'

'He won't have another chance to break loose, not with the door padlocked and one of the boys on guard day and night.'

Stagg nodded, his expression thoughtful. 'There's something I forgot to mention about that Slade feller. Like I said I was kind of dozin', not payin' much attention at first. He was awful slow forkin' saddle ... stood there between his bronc and your buck horse like he was fussin' with his saddle.' The liveryman was suddenly reining his team to a standstill. 'Maybe I'm crazy, but I'm thinkin' of the time awhile back when some skunk cut your saddle girth.'

'I'm taking a look.' Mark slid from his seat and hurried to the buckskin trailing on his lead-rope. Stagg heard an angry exclamation.

'You guessed right, Jim. The cinch is sliced to a close inch.'

Mark stripped off the saddle, flung it over the wheel to the rear seat and resumed his place by the liveryman's side.

Stagg sent the team into a fast trot. 'The feller wasn't figgerin' you'd be ridin' into town with me,' he said.

'I've an idea he's waiting on the trail I'd have taken for the ranch.' Angry speculation was in Mark's eyes. 'He'd have trailed me, waited for my saddle to turn, shot me like a sitting duck.'

'And you wearin' no gun,' Jim Stagg reminded him. 'You sure would have been a dead duck. Mighty careless of you – forgetting your gun.'

'We don't wear guns to a friend's funeral.'

'I'll loan you a .45 when we get to the barn,' Stagg said. 'No tellin' what you'll run into in town.'

'I'll be looking for the man who cut my saddle cinch,' Mark said grimly. 'The man riding Reeve Bett's red roan.'

Slade was already in Bett's office when

Stagg and Mark passed up the street on the way to the livery barn. The renegade swore softly when he realised the trailing buckskin was not wearing a saddle.

'I was up the trail always, waiting for Hudson to show up,' he told Bett. 'He fooled me, climbed in with old Stagg and headed for town with his bronc on a lead-rope.' Slade looked pointedly at the desk drawer. 'I could do with a drink.'

Bett shook his head, changed his mind, reluctantly produced a bottle from the drawer. 'Glass on the shelf,' he said grumpily.

The man found the glass and poured himself a drink. *'Bueno.* Hits the spot, Boss.' He reached again for the bottle on the desk. Bett snatched it, dropped it in the drawer.

'Go easy with the stuff.' He closed the drawer, turned the key. 'I want to know what went wrong.'

Slade glowered at the empty glass. 'I was up on the hillside, saw him drive off with Stagg. The saddle was on the bronc, so he couldn't have known what I done to the cinch. Old Stagg couldn't have known either. He was dozin' there in the buckboard when I used the knife.'

'The horse wasn't wearing a saddle when they passed the office just now,' Bett said.

'It could have bust loose and fell off, and him not notice.' Slade shifted uneasily in his chair. He was not liking the ugly glitter in the other man's eyes.

'The saddle was in the buckboard,' Bett said. 'He must have found out about the cinch. Damn you, Slade. If Stagg recognised your roan horse they'll guess you did it.'

'I told you he was settin' there dozing,' mumbled the renegade. 'He wasn't noticin' nothin'.'

'Don't fool yourself,' Bett said savagely. 'Stagg knows every horse in the San Carlos. He knows I got that roan from Ed Starkey.' He considered a moment. 'Where's the horse now?'

'In your yard back of the office.'

'You've got to get him away from there in a hurry, some place out of town.'

'Sure will.' Slade got to his feet. He was in a hurry himself to get away from his poisonous little boss.

'Wait a minute.' Bett gazed at him thoughtfully. 'It's strange Cherokee hasn't shown up in town.'

'It sure is,' agreed Slade. 'He lit out awful fast when I busted him loose from that granary. I figgered he was headin' for town.'

'Didn't he tell you anything about Brice?'

There was a hint of panic in Bett's voice.

'He didn't tell me nothin'.' There was a odd gleam in the renegade's eyes. 'When I turned round from closin' the stable door he was high-tailin' it across the yard like the devil was taggin' him.'

Reeve Bett glowered at the desk drawer. He was needing a drink himself at that moment. Slade's eyes followed the look hopefully. Bett's outstretched hand fell to his knee. He shook his head impatiently.

'I've got a job for you,' he said. 'Get out to the Brice ranch and find out if he and his girl are still there. You should be back here by sunset.'

'I savvy.' Slade's disappointed look was on the desk drawer.

'Put your saddle on that grey horse in the barn that wears no brand. Take the roan with you and turn him loose out of town. He'll find his way back to Starkey's ranch.'

'I savvy.' Slade hesitated. 'It's a long ride over to the Brice ranch. I reckon I'll step over the hotel and have a bite first.'

'You're not showing yourself on the street,' almost snarled Bett. 'Not while Hudson's in town. He'll be looking for you with a gun.'

'I sure got to eat,' grumbled the man.

Bett was suddenly his smiling, suave self

again. He unlocked the desk drawer and reached for the bottle. 'Have a drink while I see about some food for you,' he said. He went to the rear door of the office. He opened it, spoke to an elderly Mexican who was washing the red-wheeled buggy in the yard.

'Manuel – run across to the hotel and have them wrap some sandwiches. Bring them back to the stable on the run. I'm in a hurry.'

'*Si, Señor–*' The Mexican dropped his sponge in the bucket and turned hastily towards the gate opening into the alley between the office and the Roundup Saloon.

Bett closed the door and returned to his desk where Slade was again reaching for the bottle. Bett shook his head, returned the bottle to the drawer.

'You heard me,' he said. 'Get out to the barn fast and throw your saddle on the grey. The Mex will be back with the sandwiches by the time you're ready to leave, and don't forget the roan. Turn him loose when you get a couple of miles from town.'

'I savvy.' The renegade wiped his mouth with shirtsleeve, hitched up sagging gun belt. 'I'll see you come sundown, Boss.'

'Make sure nobody sees you leave,' Bett warned.

'I'll head down the alley into the barranca back of the barn,' Slade reassured him.

He crossed the yard to the stable, unaware of the pair of eyes watching from behind the tangle of shrubs near the office window.

Fidel Cota waited until the man had disappeared inside the barn, then cautiously edged closer to the window. Satisfied the screening vines completely concealed him from a chance look, he continued his patient watch on the man inside.

Reeve Bett leaned back in his desk chair, fingers nervously toying with his moustache. Cherokee's disappearance worried him. From the little he had learned from Slade, the half-breed must have been wounded during an encounter with Mark Hudson and taken prisoner. It was possible Cherokee had made a second attempt to get Hudson, an attempt that had back-fired, resulted in his capture by the man he had been sent to kill.

The explanation only increased Bett's perturbations. It meant the half-breed had not fulfilled his mission at the Brice ranch. Brice was still there, alive, an ever-increasing menace.

He glanced at the rear window. The vines outside effectively screened it. No need to draw the shade there. He went to the rear door, opened it, saw Slade riding from the yard, the packet of sandwiches tied to his saddle, the roan horse trailing on a lead-rope. He closed the door, slid the bolt, locking it, and returned to the desk.

A rattle of the front door-knob, followed by a sharp rap, held him rigid. He heard Jim Stagg's voice. 'I reckon he ain't in. Mark ... door's locked and shades drawn. Let's try the hotel – have a look inside the Roundup as we pass.' Footsteps fading up the board walk... Silence.

Bett relaxed, was suddenly busy. He pushed the desk chair aside and pulled the Navajo rug from under the desk. Down on his knees, he pried up a section of floor-board with a piece of flat steel, revealing a long tin box. He opened it, gazing gloatingly at the stacks of gold coin, the neatly-tied envelopes. He counted out fifteen twenty dollar pieces, pocketed them and carefully reinserted the floor-board.

Bett got to his feet, dusted his knees, re-placed the Navajo rug and slid the chair back to the desk. He resumed his seat. It was time to do some hard thinking – plan his next move. He must remain invisible for the moment. He must not risk a public scene with Mark Hudson, a scene that could draw attention to him if the young rancher suffered a mysterious and fatal accident later... It meant waiting in the office until Hudson left town, or until sundown – and darkness. *Sundown*. Slade had said he would be back from the Brice ranch at sundown. He wanted to know if Brice was dead, or had heeded the warning and fled with is daughter. He would soon know. The thought tingled him.

Bett rose from his chair and crossed the office to the couch. He would lie down, take it easy, while he waited.

A scraping of the vines outside the rear window drew his attention. 'A vagrant gust of wind,' he decided as he stretched out on the couch.

CHAPTER TEN

Fidel Cota crouched behind the heavy tangle of vines, motionless as a frightened rabbit hiding from a coyote. He was in a tight spot, he realised, as he watched the Mexican sponging the red-wheeled buggy in the yard.

Fidel's thoughts raced. Discovery would be fatal – prevent him from carrying vitally important news to his boss, almost surely result in his own sudden death. It was a time for cool thinking.

His keen ears had picked up much of the conversation between Bett and the desperado who had ridden away with the roan horse on a lead-rope. The news of Mark Hudson's arrival in town increased his impatience to get away, a difficult problem because of the man in the yard.

He had managed to watch Bett's odd behaviour in the office after Slade's departure – the drawing of the shades, the removal of the floor-board under which something was apparently concealed. A secret cache, he guessed. It would all greatly interest his boss – this evidence that would mean the hangman's rope for Reeve Bett.

Fidel peered cautiously through the screening leaves. The man was pushing the buggy into the lean-to shed against the barn. He tensed himself for a stealthy run to the alley gate. The Mexican closed the shed door, stood for a minute, rolling a cigarette, gaze idling around the yard, resting briefly on the vine-screened window. He lit the cigarette and slouched into the stable.

Fidel hesitated. He was not liking that momentary look at the tangle of vines behind which he crouched. Summoning his courage, he crawled out. A dry branch crackled under foot. Too late for retreat, Fidel streaked across the yard for the alley gate. Footsteps raced after him, a hand grabbed his arm as he reached for the latch – a knife pressed into his back.

Fidel stood rigid, too dismayed to even turn his head for a look at his captor.

'I thought I heard something stir in those vines,' the Mexican said in Spanish. He jerked Fidel around, peered into his face. 'I fooled you, pretended to have business in the stable.'

'I was looking for a job,' Fidel was thinking fast. 'Nobody here when I came, so I thought the vines would shade me from the sun while I waited. I went to sleep.'

'A nice story,' jeered the Mexican. 'You came to steal, or to spy. I must lock you up while I go and tell my boss about you.' He gestured towards the barn with the long-bladed knife.

His young shoulders drooping, Fidel allowed himself to be propelled into the darkness of the barn. It was senseless to resist against the menace of that wicked knife.

Manuel opened the door of what was evidently a small storage room for grain. Again he motioned with the knife. Fidel reluctantly stepped inside, felt a hand roughly shove him. He sprawled headlong on a pile of empty sacks. 'My boss will talk to you later,' the man said. The door closed. Fidel heard the click of a bolt.

Fidel lay for a few moments listening to the man's retreating footsteps. He got to his feet, gazed hopelessly around his dark, windowless little prison. His heart sank. It seemed the finish. He had failed his boss, and his own life would soon pay for the failure. Reeve Bett would recognise him, and guess why he had been hiding in the tangle of vines over the window. His stricken eyes fastened on a wide crack in one of the rough boards that walled the storage room. Sunlight streamed through the crack. Fidel gazed at it. He was remembering he had been marched to the far end of the barn before reaching the door of his prison. Beyond the wall with the split board would be the barranca Slade had mentioned, winding through the chaparral west of the town.

The tiny bit of sunlight seemed to beckon him, revive faltering hope. He sank on his knees by the board, fingered the split which ran diagonally across its width. It was a wide board, wide enough for him to squeeze through if he could pry it loose. He began to grope around in the darkness for a tool, something small enough to insert in the crack, yet strong enough to use as a lever.

Manuel mounted the step to the rear of the office. Bett heard his knock, lay motionless on the couch. While Mark Hudson was in town he was keeping out of sight. He was not wanting it known he was in his office.

The Mexican knocked again. No response. He stood there for a moment, a puzzled look on his face. He had seen the boss peering from the door when Slade rode away. He must have gone out, perhaps to the Roundup, or over to the hotel.

Manuel muttered an oath, made his way to the alley gate. Nothing to do but find his boss and tell him about the young snake he had caught hiding under the vines.

He looked in the saloon. His boss was not there, but one of the several men lined up at the bar recognised him, a fellow compatriot from below the border. Manuel accepted his invitation to join him in a drink to their meeting. Manuel felt impelled to return the hospitality, finally left the Roundup with four drinks of whisky under his belt.

Manuel crossed the street to the hotel. He was feeling pretty good now, not caring much if he didn't find his boss.

He climbed the steps to the hotel porch where Jim Stagg, emerging from the lobby with Mark, recognised him.

'We're looking for your boss, Manuel,' the liveryman said. 'He's not in his office, and he's not here. We tried the Roundup, too.'

The Mexican grinned owlishly at him. 'No – not in office. I try find *Señor* Bett ... no can find.'

'Sure is queer where he got to,' Jim Stagg said. 'Looks like he went off some place with Starkey, like the barman figgered.'

Manuel was not liking the way the liveryman's friend was looking at him. He had reasons to fear strangers who seemed too interested in him. The gringo might be a law officer. His whisky-confused mind sensed danger. He turned abruptly and went lurching across the street back to the saloon. He needed another drink, several drinks, and anyway *Señor* Stagg had said his boss was not in the hotel.

Mark's gaze followed him thoughtfully. 'Who is he, Jim? He was scared of me.'

'He ain't been in town long,' Stagg said. 'Works for Bett – stableman. A bad hombre from below the border.'

'We should have asked about the roan,' Mark said.

'We can take a look in the barn back of Bett's office while he's in the saloon,' Jim suggested.

They crossed the street and turned into the alley to the yard gate.

'No roan horse here,' Jim Stagg said, after a brief look inside the stable. 'Only Bett's buggy team.'

They peered into the lean-to shed. 'Bett's buggy,' Mark observed. 'Just been washed. I wonder what's become of the man.'

'He likely went off some place with Ed Starkey,' guessed Stagg.

122

Their repeated knocks on the back door brought no response. 'He just ain't here,' Stagg said as they pushed through the yard into the alley.

The voices, the knocks on the office door, faintly reached Fidel, crouching near the loosened wall board in the little store room at the far end of the barn. He kept very still, hardly daring to breathe, his heart pounding. The fierce old Mexican was back. It was the end. No chance now to escape. Silence at last. His fears subsided and he resumed his stealthy attack on the broken board.

Unaware they had been so close to the missing Fidel, his friends paused at the sheriff's office on their way back to the livery barn. The office was still closed.

'I reckon he's with Reeve Bett and Starkey some place,' surmised Stagg. 'Him and Bett is awful chummy these days. Corter ain't the man he used to be before Bett hit this town.'

'I've noticed the change,' Mark said. 'I've an idea he's nothing more than Bett's hired man.'

'When a feller has a weak spot it shows up when he needs cash like he does,' philosophised the liveryman. 'Him and Ed Starkey both have their feet in Bett's trough.'

Disappointment awaited them at the livery barn. Neither of the hostlers had seen Fidel Cota. Mark's concern grew.

They went down the hill, back to the livery barn. Mark's concern for Fidel's safety was increasing with every passing moment.

He hurriedly saddled the buckskin. 'There's a chance he's already on his way back to the ranch,' he told Stagg.

The liveryman shook his head. 'He wouldn't go off and not leave word here.'

'He could have left word with his uncle in Old Town,' Mark said. 'I'll soon find out if he's been seen at the *cantina*.'

'If he shows up at the barn I'll see that he gets back to the ranch safe,' Jim Stagg promised. 'I'll take him back myself.'

Manuel had by now returned to the little store room, and was gazing with frightened eyes at the pushed-out board. His prisoner had escaped, and there would be hell to pay if his boss learned about it.

The Mexican rubbed the bristles of his unshaved chin. He was not feeling so good after his several more drinks with his old friend from below the border. One important fact loomed in his bemused mind. His boss must not learn about the young prowler he had nabbed in the yard and locked up in the store room.

Fidel reached a thick clump of greasewood and burrowed under the branches from sight of possible eyes. He had a decision to make and must do some thinking. He could not risk showing himself in town – be seen at Stagg's Livery and Feed Stables. Enemy eyes might spot him, betray his presence to Reeve Bett. No – it would be unwise to return to the barn. Jim Stagg and Mark would be wondering what had become of him, but better to let them wonder than be captured again. His best plan would be to get his horse from his Uncle Juan Moraga's barn in Old Town and get back to the ranch.

Shadows filled the barranca as the sun dipped below the distant mountain ridge. A rider appeared on the trail below Fidel's clump of greasewood. He lay very still. The same man who had talked to Bett in the office, the same grey horse he had ridden away from the yard. He had kept his word, was back at sundown from the Brice ranch.

Fidel's eyes hardened. He longed for a gun just then. He would have liked to shoot the killer from his saddle. He could only clench his fists, watch the grey horse and rider vanish up the barranca towards the alley leading to Bett's back yard.

Reeve Bett, keeping surreptitious watch at his shade-drawn windows, saw Mark ride past. He could not be certain the rancher was leaving town. He might be heading for Old Town in a final attempt to locate the roan horse.

A rap on the back door, Slade's voice, jerked him to his feet. He unlocked the door. Slade stepped inside, spurs rasping as he crossed the room to a chair. Bett slid the bolt and followed him to the desk, dropped into his swivel chair.

'Well?' His bright eyes were fiercely questioning.

The desperado gave him a sour grin. 'I'm cravin' a drink.'

Bett unlocked the drawer, handed out the flask. Not bothering with a glass, Slade tipped the bottle to his lips.

'Was sure needin' it,' he sighed, slamming the emptied flask on the desk.

'I'm needing your report,' Bett said acidly.

'Nobody there at the ranch house,' Slade told him. 'It looks like they've skipped ... clothes gone ... horses gone ... wagon gone ... only a buggy left in the yard.'

It was not the news Bett was hoping to hear. It was evident that Cherokee had failed a second time, allowed Brice to escape. No wonder the half-breed had himself fled rather than return to town.

Bett's fingers drummed an annoyed tattoo on the desk. The warning to get out or be burned out, was a mistake. Brice should have had no warning – only a bullet fired from ambush. Only one thing to do, now. Brice must be followed. It wouldn't be difficult to pick up his trail.

He outlined his plan to Slade. 'Take Curly Joe with you and be on your way at sunup.'

'I reckon we can pick up the trail easy,' the desperado said. An ugly grin twisted his lips. 'What'll we do with the gal?'

'I don't care what you do with her,' Bett's tone was callous. 'Just make sure she never gets back to San Carlos.'

'She's a purty piece of goods.' Slade's eyes gleamed. 'I reckon we can take care of her, Boss.'

'See that you do.' Bett paused. 'There's a hundred dollars waiting for each of you when you get back with proof that Brice is dead.'

Slade nodded. 'I savvy–' He chuckled, rolling amused eyes at Bett. 'That Mex of yours was snorin' his head off in his bunk when I put the grey bronc in the barn. Soused to the eyes.'

'He wasn't around when Stagg and Hudson came snooping in the barn.'

'Over at the bar, tankin' up,' guessed Slade.

'It's lucky they didn't run into him in the barn,' Bett said. The thought sent a cold prickle down his spine. 'Manuel would have let it slip about the roan.'

'You sure acted plenty smart about that bronc,' admired the desperado. He got to his feet, patted his lean stomach. 'I'm headin' for the Chinaman's and fill up on steak and pie. Lost them damn sandwiches somewheres on the trail. I'm sure hungry.'

Bett's lifted hand stopped him. 'We've got to make sure Hudson has left town before you show yourself on the street.'

'He ain't in town no more,' Slade said. 'I seen him and his buck horse two miles out ... spotted 'em from the ridge in time to take cover.'

'Fine,' Bett said, 'that's just fine. Buy yourself a drink ... tell Nick it's on the house.'

'*Gracias.*' Slade took his customary hitch at gun-belt and turned to the back door. He never used the street entrance.

Bett's voice halted him at the door. 'Tell Rengo and the Pecos Kid I want to see them in a hurry.'

'I'll do that,' promised the desperado with

128

an understanding grin. The door closed behind him.

Bett got out of his chair, slid up the window shades and unlocked the door. The onrushing night was not more dark than the thoughts churning in him.

CHAPTER ELEVEN

Sunset fires were fading on the mountain ridge when Mark rode from Old Town and turned into the trail for the ranch. Deepening shadows filled canyons and gullies. Juan Moraga's warning of a possible ambush was in his mind. He kept eyes and ears alert. Bushes and rocks took on sinister shapes in the tricky twilight. Once he thought he glimpsed a rider skylined on a nearby ridge. He reined in for a minute, decided that what he had seen was a fallen tree.

He pushed on, eager to get to the ranch – and Ellen Brice. Despite his worry about Fidel, she was uppermost in his mind. If he had not allowed his thoughts to stray to her he would have heard the hoofbeats closing in behind him. A bullet screamed past, followed by the reverberating report of a rifle. He jumped his horse behind a clump of pinons, slid from his saddle and lay prone behind a fallen tree.

Silence, and then the murmur of voices near the bend in the trail.

'Looks like your bullet knocked him from the saddle, Rengo ... can see his bronc down in the bushes.'

Mark's fingers tightened on his gun. It was difficult to see in that shadow-filled light. A rock, a dead stump, could be a man standing there. He dared not risk a shot, draw their fire.

A new sound broke the stillness, the throbbing thud of hoofbeats down the trail. He heard a startled oath.

'Somebody coming up fast ... let's git out of here!'

The hasty scramble of booted feet in flight, the creak of saddle leather, a shadowy glimpse of snorting horses on the dead run up the trail. Rifle shots – the scream of a horse smothered by the roar of tumbling boulders.

Mark was on his feet, a hand reaching for his buckskin's bridle. He knew what had happened. One of his attackers had plunged over the precipice at the upper bend. He knew, too, that Juan Moraga's foresight had saved him from disaster.

Two riders raced up the trail from the lower bend, vague shapes in the near darkness. His voice halted them.

'Ramon – Felipe!'

He could see them peering down at him, rifles in their hands.

'*Por Dios!*' one of them exclaimed. 'He is not dead!'

'You were just in time,' Mark told them in Spanish. He led his horse up the bank and climbed into his saddle. From far above them came the sound of shod hoofs fading up the trail. The Mexicans' swarthy faces wore wide smiles.

'One of them got away,' regretted Felipe.

'The other one went over the cliff,' Ramon said in a satisfied voice.

'He would be dead before they hit the rocks below,' Felipe said. 'Your bullet did not miss, Ramon. He was reeling in the saddle when his horse went over.'

'You saved my life,' Mark told them gratefully.

'*Es nada,*' the Mexicans replied in unison. They sheathed their rifles.

'I think there will be no more trouble,' Mark said. 'You can return to Old Town now.'

'We ride with you all the way,' Felipe announced. 'It is the wish of *Señor* Moraga.'

'He has ordered us to guard you day and night,' added Ramon. 'We do not disobey *Señor* Moraga. He would have our ears.'

Mark saw that argument would be futile, also the idea appealed to him. The presence of these two resolute Mexicans on the ranch meant greater safety for Ellen.

They reached the upper bend where the horse had carried his rider over the precipice. Mark reined the buckskin to a halt. A sheer drop of some three hundred feet to the bottom of the gorge.

Felipe echoed his thoughts. 'They are very dead,' the Mexican said.

Mark's thoughts were grim as they continued up the trail. It could have been himself lying dead on the rugged slope. The attempt on his life indicated that Reeve Bett must have been keeping close watch on him in town. He had cunningly evaded a meeting, was probably hiding in his office during the search. He must have seen Mark leave town and sent his hired gunmen to trail him, finish the job Slade had failed to do. The man's determination appalled him, made him decide not to tell Sheriff Corter of the affair. Corter was not to be trusted where Reeve Bett was concerned. He disliked the thought of leaving the dead man in the gorge, food for the buzzards, but to inform the sheriff could prove disastrous, make himself liable to the charge of murder. If

133

Reeve Bett pulled the strings Corter would not hesitate to arrest him, throw him in jail.

Mark's decision hardened. The sheriff would learn nothing from him about the dead man. He would leave it to the slain desperado's companion to break the news of the fiasco to Bett who might decide to keep silent about the affair. He was shrewd and would not care to admit to any private knowledge that might involve him. It would be different if the sheriff went to him with Mark's story.

Mark's summing up of the situation was not far wrong. Early morning found Reeve Bett in his office, a sour look on his face as he listened to confessions of failure.

'We seen him tumble from his saddle when I shot,' Rengo said. 'We figgered he was dead and while we was lookin' to make sure, these other fellers come up fast and started shootin'. We got away from there but not quick enough. A bullet got Pecos Kid, or his bronc. Anyway they went over the cliff. I kept goin' and that's all I know, Boss.'

'Do you know who these men were?' Bett asked.

'I wasn't stoppin' to say howdy to 'em,' growled the desperado. 'Gettin' too dark, anyway.'

'Looks like that Hudson feller wears a

charm,' Slade broke in. He sat sprawled in a chair, fingers wrapped over a whisky flask, his gaunt face a mask of weariness. 'I'm fed up chasin' ghosts,' he complained. 'Me and Curly sure wore ourselves out tryin' to pick up sign of Brice and his gal. Curly can follow a woodtick in the dark of the moon, but he sure couldn't pick up sign of nothin'.'

Bett leaned back in his chair, his expression thoughtful. 'Listen, Rengo... Keep quiet about last night. Not a word to anybody about what happened to the Pecos Kid. You just don't know where he is or where he's gone, if anybody asks.'

'I savvy.' Rengo got out of his chair, a lean-hipped sandy-haired man with light blue eyes that for the moment held frank distaste as he gazed down at his deadly little boss. 'You mean you're leavin' the Pecos Kid lay there – for the buzzards?'

'You don't know where he is or where he's gone,' repeated Bett, a threat in his voice. His lip lifted in a callous smile. 'The buzzards will spread the news soon enough, and then it's up to the sheriff.'

'I ain't likin' it much,' muttered the outlaw. 'Pecos was my pal. We was kids together in Abilene.' His eyes wavered under Bett's menacing stare. He shrugged, turned to the yard door. 'Well – I reckon the sheriff will find him, like you say, Boss.'

Bett's vitriolic gaze followed him until the door closed. His look went to Slade. 'Rengo's softer than I thought,' he said.

Slade shrugged. 'Him and Pecos was awful close.' He took another pull at the flask.

'I've no use for a soft man. A soft man can talk – more trouble.'

'What do you want me to do with him?'

'Send him to the Hideout Camp as quick as he can fork a saddle. I want him a long way from town. Send Gus Silver with him and tell Gus to make sure Rengo stays there until they push the herd across the border.'

'Countin' them two hundred Bar H steers there's most a thousand head ready for the drive,' his lieutenant estimated. He grinned, reached for the flask. 'Some clean-up, Boss.'

'Go easy on the whisky,' warned Bett. 'Give me a few more days and you can drink yourself blind for all I care.'

'Whisky don't hurt me none,' growled the rustler. He got out of his chair. 'Well, I'll get Rengo and Gus started for the camp and then I'm hittin' the hay.'

Bett's voice halted him at the back door. 'Tell Manuel I'll want the buggy ready right away.'

'I'll do that,' Slade said as the door closed behind him.

Bett remained motionless in his desk chair. There was much to think about, more spinning of the sinister web that until now had successfully enmeshed his victims. Mark Hudson had again eluded him, and Samuel Brice was still alive, an ever constant menace to be destroyed.

His thoughts went to Lucy Swan, his plan to call on her at the ranch that morning. She was a pretty butterfly, easy enough to entangle in the same web that had caught her father, left him lifeless.

Bett went to a closet and opened the door, smirked at his reflection in the full-length mirror on the inside, fingered his neat vandyke, the short-cropped moustache – an elegant figure of a man to impress a girl like Lucy Swan.

He picked up his hat, made sure the street door was locked and stepped out to the back yard, closing and locking the door behind him.

Manuel had the team of bay trotters hitched to the buggy. Bett climbed in, gathered the reins. 'Don't get drunk again while I'm gone,' he warned.

'I no dreenk one leetle drop, *Señor.*'

137

'Keep an eye on things here,' he said, as he drove through the gates the Mexican swung open for him.

Lucy Swan sat on a bench shaded by a chinaberry tree in the patio, thinking of Mark Hudson. She would have to do something about it – get the girl and her father away from there.

A look of cold calculation crept into her eyes, tightened her soft lips. There *was* something she could do. She got up from the bench and walked slowly along the path towards the garden gate.

Lucy leaned over the gate. Two cowboys, perched on the corral fence, were indulging in loud-voiced sarcasm as they watched the attempts of a third man to mount a fractious colt. Their voices hushed at sight of the slim girl in her black dress. They had helped bury her father only the day before and loud jesting was unseemly in her presence.

Lucy was quite oblivious of them. Her thoughts were racing. Yes, despite Teresa Cota's warning, there was something she could do. She had a weapon that would destroy Ellen Brice's ambition to be the mistress of the great Bar H ranch. She had made no promise to keep silent about Mark's secret. She could let it be known that he was hiding the Brices in his house. She wasn't sure what his reason was for hiding them, but it must be that he was hiding them from the law. She could tell Sheriff Corter about them, make him promise not to betray her perfidy to Mark.

Her head lifted in a look across the yard at a red-wheeled buggy whirling up the avenue behind a pair of tall bay trotters. Surprise widened her eyes. Reeve Bett! He had attended the funeral the day before, and now he was back again.

Lucy turned hurriedly away. She was not sure she wanted to see the man, was inclined to tell Jenny to inform him she was not at home to callers.

Then a thought was suddenly large in her mind. He was a close friend of Sheriff Corter. Lucy's lips tightened. *Sheriff Corter*. Her chance had come! Yes – she would see Reeve Bett.

The click of the gate-latch made the decision for her, left no time for further debate. Reeve Bett was approaching down the walk. Lucy gave him a properly sad little smile.

Reeve Bett removed his hat. 'One of the men in the yard told me I'd probably find you here in the patio,' he said. His smile was gravely sympathetic. 'A very sad time for you, my dear Miss Swan. I – well I came to see if there's anything I can do to help.'

'Thank you.' She made room for him on the bench. 'You are very kind, Mr Bett.'

'I had the deepest respect for your father, Miss Swan. A fine man. His untimely death means a great loss to all of us.'

'He had many friends,' Lucy said. She was thinking to herself. *Now's my chance to make it seem natural.* 'Mark Hudson would be here at this moment, only he has so much on his mind. You know Mark, don't you, Mr Bett? He's a particular friend of mine.'

'Of course I know him.' Bett's tone was guarded. Her mention of Mark Hudson somewhat disconcerted him, gave him an uneasy moment. 'Are you expecting him, Miss Swan?'

Lucy shook her head sadly. 'No ... he can't get away, or he would be here now. You see, he has a wounded man and his daughter in the house and is quite worried about them.'

Bett managed to keep his voice casual. 'Friends of his, I suppose?'

'Well – not exactly *friends*. I think Mr Brice has a small ranch somewhere near Mark's place. Mark found him badly wounded, shot, I think, and took him and the girl over to Bar H. The girl, Ellen, is quite pathetic, poor thing.'

'Ah, yes–' Bett appeared to be searching his mind. 'Brice you say the name is? Yes, Sam Brice. I've heard of him.'

'There's talk he's a cow-thief – a rustler,' Lucy said with a nervous little laugh. 'I can't imagine why Mark would hide a rustler in his house.'

'It does seem strange.' Bett's tone was grave.

'I think Mark doesn't want Sheriff Corter to know about it,' Lucy said.

'I'm afraid the sheriff wouldn't like it.' Bett kept his gaze on the pigeons. He did not want her to see the unholy glitter in his eyes.

Lucy's show of alarm was well done. She sat up, frantic appeal in her voice. 'Oh, you mustn't tell Sheriff Corter. It's a secret. Mark would never forgive me.'

'It's a serious matter,' Bett said. 'I think Sheriff Corter should know.'

'I suppose he should,' she reluctantly agreed. 'But Mr Bett, please, please don't let *anyone* know that I told you. Mark would never forgive me.'

'You have my promise,' Bett assured her smoothly. He got to his feet. 'Well, Miss Swan ... I must be on my way. I just wanted you to know that I'm always glad to be of help.'

Lucy accompanied him to the gate, stood watching until the red-wheeled buggy disappeared down the avenue. *I've done it,* she exulted. *Ellen Brice will soon be out of Mark's house and he'll never know I did it.*

She walked slowly back to the bench near the fountain, her chin triumphantly high, her eyes sparkling. Reeve Bett would be surprised if he knew she was using him as a tool to destroy a hated rival. He was an odious little man. She wondered what had been the real reason for his visit.

A chill stole through Lucy as she sat there on the bench thinking of Reeve Bett, thinking of what she had done.

CHAPTER TWELVE

Pat Race stood framed in the lighted door-way of the bunkhouse, thoughtfully shaping a cigarette. There was reason for the heavy frown on his face. He was foreman of Bar H and the loss of two hundred prime steers rankled in him. He felt that he had failed his boss and his spirits were low. He was restless, wanted action. It had been a long day, waiting for Mark's return from Bill Swan's funeral.

The sound of hoofbeats rapidly approaching up the avenue brought his hands to his gun-butts.

'The boss,' Pat recognised, as three riders emerged from the darkness of the tree-lined avenue. 'Has two fellers with him.'

They continued on their way to the garden gate. Pat Race was already hurrying across the yard.

Mark swung from his saddle, turned the buckskin over to Tulsa who emerged hastily from the barn. 'Brought some help back with me,' he said. 'I think you know them, Pat.'

'I sure do.' There was approval in the smile the foreman gave the two Mexicans. *'Coma'sta,'* he greeted.

'Coma'sta, Señor,' they replied in unison.

'Teresa will look after you in the kitchen,' Mark told them. 'I'll see you later.'

'Never could tell them twins apart,' Pat Race said as the two Mexicans followed Tulsa to the barn with their horses.

'Felipe always wears a red band around his sombrero,' Mark informed him. 'Ramon wears a yellow one.'

'I wouldn't be rememberin' them colours,' chuckled the foreman. His face sobered. 'Fidel Cota got in about an hour ago ... seemed awful excited ... wouldn't tell us nothing. Said he had big news and would only tell it to you.'

'Thank God!' Mark exclaimed fervently. 'Jim Stagg and I have been looking all over town for him.'

'The kid looked awful tired,' the foreman said. 'I reckon he's had a tough time of it.'

Alamo Jones joined them, on his way from the granary to the bunkhouse, a tall, gaunt man with the shambling stride of a mountain man which he had been in earlier years before joining the Bar H outfit.

Pat Race gave him an inquiring look as he

shambled up, an ancient Sharps rifle tucked under an arm. 'How's the feller?'

'Doin' fine sence you and the boss fixed up his arm,' Alamo informed him. 'Swellin' is most gone.'

'Fine,' Mark said. 'He'll maybe do some talking soon.'

Alamo shook his head. 'He's a tough humbre. I met up with him one time in San Antone ... name of Cherokee, a no-good breed and all pizen.'

'At least we know his name even if he won't talk,' Mark said.

Alamo gnawed reflectively on a plug of tobacco. 'Turn him over to me and Bearcat,' he suggested. 'We savvy ways to make a feller talk plenty.' He went on his way to the bunkhouse.

Mark was impatient now to get to the house. Fidel Cota had 'big' news for him, and looming large in his mind was the thought of Ellen Brice. Something in the foreman's manner held his step. He knew Pat and sensed an urgency in him.

'All right,' he said. 'What is it, Pat?'

'It's them steers!' exploded the foreman. 'I figger we should go after 'em and right soon. Hate like hell to lose 'em to them damn rustlers.'

'We're awfully tied up right now, Pat.'

'I'm wantin' to head back to Willow Creek ... take Jerico and Brazos with me.'

Mark shook his head. 'I'm needing all of you here,' he objected. He considered a moment. 'Let it ride until morning, Pat. Maybe we can work out some plan then.'

'It's up to you,' reluctantly assented the foreman. 'You're the boss.'

'That's right.' Mark softened the curt retort with an affectionate slap on the back. 'And don't forget that you're the boss's right hand, Pat. We'll talk it over in the morning.'

He went on his way, a sense of haste lengthening his stride. A glimpse of Ellen, and then Fidel. He had refrained from telling Pat Race about the attempted ambush. For the present it was best that only himself and the two Mexicans knew about the man lying dead in the gorge. If the sheriff came storming up with his posse, Pat could truthfully say it was all news to him.

Teresa Cota intercepted him in the hall, relief mixed with disapproval in her handsome eyes. 'You have been gone so long, Markito. I was worried. You did not tell me you were going to town after the funeral.'

'How do you know I've been in town?'

'Fidel told me, of course.'

146

'I looked all over for him in town,' Mark said, a hint of pique in his voice. 'He must have been hiding from me.'

'He must have had a good reason,' defended Fidel's grandmother. 'The poor boy ... he was about dead when he came – starving for food.' She shook a finger at him. 'I fear the job you gave him to do in town was very dangerous, Markito.'

Mark said wearily, 'I warned him it might be dangerous. Even so, you've a right to blame me.'

Teresa relented. 'No, no, Markito! The blame is mine for boasting of Fidel's smartness.' Pride glowed in her eyes. 'He *is* smart – and brave like his great-grandfather.' She nodded her head. 'And loyal to the last drop of his blood. He has news, but refuses to talk, says it is for your ears alone.'

'I'll see him in a few minutes,' Mark promised. 'And Teresa, I've brought Ramon and Felipe Escobar back with me. They'll be seeing you in the kitchen soon.'

'Those twins?' A smile wreathed the housekeeper's face. *'Madre de Dios!* Delfina will lose what little mind she has. She is Felipe's adored little pigeon.' Flapping her hands, Teresa scurried off to her kitchen.

Mark hung his hat and gun-belt on the

hall rack and stood for a moment, gazing irresolutely down the hall at Ellen's bedroom door. Teresa had given him no time to ask about the Brices. The door to Sam Brice's room opened.

She stood there, hesitant, a warning finger on her lips. 'I heard you talking to Teresa.'

He was at her side in a moment. 'Ellen!'

His look, the vibrant whisper of her name, brought colour to her cheeks.

'He's asleep,' she whispered back.

'Yes – yes, but–'

Her hand continued to warn him off. 'I must talk to you. It's important.'

Mark hesitated, gestured down the hall. She followed him into the ranch-office. He closed the door, turned, his arms reaching for her. Ellen eluded the embrace, sank into a chair.

She hid her face with both hands under his devouring look. 'Please ... I can't bear it. You mustn't look at me like that ... make – make me weak.'

'I don't understand,' Mark said, unhappily. 'You have been in my thoughts ever since I left this morning. You must know I love you, Ellen.'

Her hands dropped to her lap, and for a fleeting instant heaven looked from her eyes. She shook her head. 'You are making it so hard for me, Mark. There are reasons why you mustn't love me. That other girl, Lucy Swan, is the one for you. She's crazy about you and that's why she couldn't bear to stay here under the same roof with me.'

Mark frowned. 'Teresa's been talking.'

'I didn't need any talk from Teresa to realise I'm an interloper here.'

'You're not an interloper,' Mark said violently. 'You are the girl I love and want to marry – if you'll have me.'

'No, no!' She freed herself, hands pushing him away. 'You wouldn't – if you knew what father wants to tell you.'

'I don't care what your father tells me, I love you, Ellen, and want you.' He drew her close again. 'You love me, too, Ellen. No matter what you say, I know you love me.'

For a moment her arms stole around his neck, then again she pushed him away. 'No, no! Wait until father tells you something you have a right to know about us.' Before he could stop her she opened the door and fled into the hall.

Mark made no attempt to follow. He dropped into his desk chair, gazed gloomily at the wall map of the Bar H. Of what use was the ranch to him if Ellen couldn't or wouldn't be its mistress. Bar H would be a joyless, barren wilderness without her.

Fidel then came into the office. Excitement glittered in the young Mexican's eyes. It was plain that danger had hovered uncomfortably close to him during his brief stay in town. He seemed older, his young face hardened by some grim ordeal.

Mark leaned back in his desk chair. 'All right,' he said. 'Let's have it.'

Excitement, elation, fired his own eyes as he listened to the young Mexican's account of his adventure in Reeve Bett's yard, his capture by Manuel – the escape from the storage room in the barn.

'Jim Stagg and I were there, looking for you,' Mark told him. 'If we had only known you were so near!'

'I heard voices,' Fidel said. 'I thought those devils were coming to get me ... I thought it was my finish.'

'You've been through a lot of hell.' Mark spoke remorsefully. 'I shouldn't have sent you to town, Fidel. I should have known you'd run into trouble.'

'*Es nada.*' The young Mexican's superb scorn of danger, his gesture, were so imitative of old Fernando Cota that Mark wanted to smile. 'My great-grandfather once told me

150

the only thing a man need fear was *fear*,' Fidel Cota said with another proud lift of his hand. 'I am a man, *Señor.*'

'You've done a man's work, all right.' Mark studied the notes he had been taking down during Fidel's recital. Jim Stagg's guess about the ownership of the roan horse was correct. Bett had hurried the horse and Slade out of town. Discovery of the roan in Bett's barn would have pointed the finger of suspicion directly at him.

Fidel's voice interrupted his reflections. 'Does what I have seen and heard please you, *Señor?* Have I brought you the proof that will hang this wicked man?'

'It's proof that convinces me,' Mark assured him. 'It's evidence that can put him in prison for a lot of years.' He thought of Bill Swan, added grimly, 'It's possible we'll find more evidence that will hang him for murder.'

'Manuel, too,' Fidel said fiercely. 'He would have cut my throat.' He got to his feet, looked at Mark pleadingly. '*Señor,* now I'm a man, I must wear a gun. If I'd had a gun I could have killed Slade when he passed me in the chaparral on his way back from the Brice ranch. He is a bad man, and would have killed *Señor* Brice if he had found him

151

at the ranch. Bett is very anxious for *Señor* Brice to die.'

'It's lucky for Brice he got away from there in time,' Mark said.

'He told Slade he could do what he wanted with *Señorita* Brice when he found her,' Fidel reminded him in a shocked voice.

'Yes, I'm remembering, and it's another nail in their coffins.' Mark's face was pale, his voice tight with the rage in him. He longed at that moment to have his fingers around Bett's throat. There would have been no need for a hangman's rope.

He saw Fidel's longing look fastened on the Colt .45 hanging on a peg near the silver-mounted saddle. He motioned at it. 'It's yours, Fidel. My father would say you are worthy to wear it.'

The youth's face glowed. '*Señor!* The Old *Señor's* gun!' He took it and the cartridge-filled holster, reverently from the peg, buckled the belt around his lean waist with trembling fingers. 'I will use it only in defence of the rancho, and you.'

'I know you will, Fidel. You have proved yourself a man these past twenty-four hours.' His hand lifted in a parting gesture. 'I'll see you in the morning, so on your toes for another job I may have for you.'

'I will be ready,' Fidel assured him, hand on the butt of his longed-for gun. The door closed behind him.

Mark relaxed in his chair, his mind busy with the problems raised by Fidel's story of what he had seen and heard while crouching in the vines under Reeve Bett's office window. The evidence against the man was in his hands, but what could he do with it? No use going to Sheriff Corter with the story. The sheriff would blandly say that Fidel was a liar and refuse to serve a warrant for Bett's arrest.

Mark sat for long minutes, focusing his thoughts that had vaguely come to him while talking to Fidel. He had realised immediately the futility of attempting any direct personal action. He would have to call for outside help, help with the teeth of the law in it, help that Sheriff Corter would be forced to respect and obey.

Slowly Mark's thoughts crystallised to decision. He would send for U.S. Deputy Marshal Ed Horne, his long-time friend. He decided against writing a letter, for fear it might be intercepted at the San Carlos post office. A trusted messenger was the best answer to the problem, which was why the thought of using Fidel Cota had filtered vaguely through his mind a few minutes earlier. Fidel could make the journey to Hatchita inside of a day. If Horne was not tied up on another job he could arrive at the ranch before a second sundown.

Mark found a sheet of paper and scrawled a message he knew would bring the Deputy Marshal on the jump. He thrust the letter in an envelope and sealed it. Early dawn would see Fidel on the way to Silver City with it. The decision cheered him enormously.

The lift was only momentary as he recalled Ellen's words. *There are reasons why you mustn't love me... Wait until father tells you something you have a right to know about us.*

Mark stirred restlessly in his chair. He wasn't frightened of any dark secret Brice felt impelled to divulge about his past. What frightened him was Ellen's mistaken belief that it was an insurmountable barrier, forever keeping them apart, worse still, destroy his love for her. She was so wrong.

He went quietly down the hall. Light showed faintly under Ellen's door. It dimmed out as he approached, a sign that she was not wanting to see him again that night. Brice's room was dark, too. He would have liked to see Brice and get it over with. He restrained the impulse to knock. Brice was an ill man. It would be heartless to awaken him.

Mark turned away. Nothing he could do about it until morning.

Morning! So much to do when morning came. He was needing sleep himself. He had never felt so weary, so depressed.

He took a look in the patio, saw Brasca and Bearcat on vigilant guard in the moonlight. Satisfied, he made his way to his own room.

From somewhere far back in the garden came the soft strumming of a guitar. Felipe, serenading his Delfina. The plaintive strains lulled him to sleep.

CHAPTER THIRTEEN

Much to Mark's surprise, early dawn found him on the trail with Pat Race and Jerico. He had awakened with the decision to accompany the foreman to the Willow Creek camp firmly in his mind. He made no attempt to see Ellen or her father before leaving. Teresa would tell them of his plans to make a search for the stolen steers. Fidel was already on his way to Hatchita with the letter to the U.S. deputy marshal. It would be at least two days before Horne arrived at the ranch. The time of waiting for the deputy marshal would be best spent in making an attempt to recover the steers.

Increasing gloom rode with him as unhappy doubts and fears churned in him. The pull of the girl he loved was almost more than he could resist. He reined his horse to a standstill, of a mind to turn back.

Pat Race looked at him curiously. 'What's wrong?' he asked.

Mark sought desperately for an excuse. 'I'm not sure we should leave the ranch, even for a day,' he said. 'Anything might happen.'

'No chance for that damn half-breed to break loose,' Pat reassured him. 'Not with one of the boys standin' watch on the granary day and night.'

'I'm thinking of Brice. Somebody may try to get at him.'

'He's safe enough,' Pat said. 'You've got him guarded like he was the U.S. Mint. Brasca and Bearcat, and Alamo and old Baldy, and them two Mex hombres, Felipe and Ramon. Hell, there ain't no chance a-tall for nobody to get at Brice.'

'All right, all right,' Mark said irritably as he started his horse. It was impossible to admit his real motive for wanting to turn back. Pat would think he was soft in the head. The foreman's arguments seemed sound, and he was easy enough in his mind about the safety of Brice and Ellen. Prowlers were due for a fatal reception if they ventured too close to the house. Nobody knew that Brice and his daughter were in hiding there, least of all, Reeve Bett.

The trail dipped over a low ridge to a meadow fed by a creek fringed with willows and now overflowing its banks after the recent storm. The bawling of cattle came to them from the corrals less than a mile distant. Smoke lifted lazily from the cookshack near the long bunkhouse where a man stood framed in the doorway. He was suddenly hurrying towards a group of riders near the horse corral. His shout faintly reached their ears as he slid into a saddle and started in their direction, horse on the run.

'Looks like Rusty is some anxious to see us,' commented Pat Race. 'He's sure comin' fast.' He spurred his own horse into a run. Mark and Jerico keeping pace with him.

The rider reined his horse to a standstill as they converged. 'I was hopin' you'd show up!' He was a competent-looking man and wore a sandy moustache that drooped over a good-humoured mouth. 'Got big news for you.'

'We figgered somethin' was eatin' you,' the foreman said with a grin. 'What's the big news that's got you all het up?'

'Howdy, Boss.' There was relief in the look Rusty Hall gave Mark. 'Answerin' your question, Pat, we done located them damn rustlers. I was about to send Salty hightailin' it to the ranch to tell you.'

'Good work, Rusty,' Mark said.

'Where is this place?' queried the foreman. 'Did you spot them Bar H steers of ours there?'

'I reckon you know where the Devil's Hideout is,' Rusty said. 'Down there in them maze of canyons west of the Brice place. They've got over a thousand head cached there, and our Bar H steers with 'em.'

Pat Race looked at Mark. 'I reckon that's all we want to know, huh, Boss?'

Mark said, briefly, 'Let's go.'

It was plain from the expectant looks on the faces of the some half score riders grouped near the horse corral, that they were eager for action. An ear-splitting yell chorused from their throats when Mark told them to make ready for a raid on the rustler's hideout.

Old Sinful, listening from the doorway of his cook-shack, waved a frying-pan at them. 'I'll fix sandwiches for you to take along. No tellin' when you'll git back.' He vanished into his little domain.

Canteens were filled and made fast to saddles, cartridge-belt replenished, rifles examined, all done with a minimum of words. There was grim purpose and efficiency in the way the Bar H men prepared for the business of making war on the hated marauders of the range. Pride welled in Mark's heart as he watched them. These Bar H men were fighters. The rustlers were due for a show-down they would never forget.

Old Sinful appeared, handing out his packets of sandwiches. He stood there in the doorway of his cook-shack, a wide grin on his leathery face as they rode away, Mark and Pat heading the contingent.

It was past noon when the trail dropped them into a treeless, boulder-strewn gorge blistering under the torrid sun. Here and there rock-ribbed depressions held pools of water left by the cloudburst. Mark reined in his horse, waited for the others, following in single file down the narrow trail. He was familiar with the intricate maze of canyons and gorges and knew they were within a mile of the rustlers' camp in the cliff-girded basin known as the Devil's Hideout.

'Here's water for our horses,' he said. 'We can eat while we do some planning.' He slid from his saddle and led the buckskin to one of the little pools and reached for his packet of sandwiches.

The riders gathered around the pool with their horses, sandwiches in hands. Jerico saw a convenient boulder and thoughtlessly sat on it. He jumped up with a pained ejaculation.

'Like to have burned the seat of my pants off me,' he grumbled.

'Ol' tenderfoot,' jeered Rusty Hall. 'You orter savvy this is hell's back-yard. Them rocks is for lizards to set on.'

Mark was studying the rugged slope to the left of the gorge. The cloudburst had gouged out a narrow chasm down the slope from the ridge above. It would be a tough climb over the tumbled boulders and debris up to the newly-torn cleft which he surmised would afford a good view of the rustler's hideout camp below.

'I reckon that's a real smart idee,' agreed Pat Race when Mark explained what was in his mind. 'No sense runnin' into a lot of hot lead if we can take 'em by surprise from behind.'

'Just the two of us,' Mark said. 'I'm not sure we can even make it to the top.'

'Sure – just me and you.' The foreman's stern gaze warned the interested cowboys. 'You fellers stick close here, and don't start nothin' on your own. Savvy?'

'We savvy,' Rusty Hall assured him. 'We ain't movin' 'til you say the word.'

They were a good half-hour making the ascent over the boulders and slippery shale. The midday sun blazed mercilessly down on them and by the time they reached the cleft they were dripping with perspiration.

They lay prone behind a jagged boulder, wiping the salty sweat from eyes with their bandannas before taking a look down into the cliff-girded meadow below.

The cattle first caught their attention. The herd had done its morning grazing and for the most was lying down near a pool fed by a spring that bubbled from the side of the cliff. They would not be stirring again until mid-afternoon when as the way with range cattle they would gradually spread out in search of the sparse grass at the far end of the basin. The only man visible was a lone rider slowly circling the somnolent herd. It was obvious his fellow-rustlers had sought relief from the blistering sun and were taking their ease in the several tents beyond the pool. No sign of life, there, except a faint haze of smoke spiralling from an elbow of stove pipe in the cook tent.

Silence lay heavy on the sweltering camp. Only an occasional bellow from the herd, the restless stamp of a fly-plagued horse in the improvised rope corral. None of the score or more horses in the corral wore saddles. The gear, including bridles and blankets was lying in disorderly heaps near the corral. It was plain the rustlers were completely unsuspecting of any possible trouble.

'We'd raise hell with 'em if we could stampede the herd *and* the remuda,' Pat Race said. 'We'd have them damn cow-thieves runnin' 'round in circles chasin' their broncs.'

'Now's the time,' agreed Mark. 'Hit them hard with a surprise attack. The big question is how can we do it?' His gaze went to the yawning mouth of a canyon that broke through the cliffs to the right of the herd. The flimsy rope-corral and the tents would be directly in the path of those thousand or more stampeding cattle.

Pat Race listened dubiously to his swiftly-conceived plan. 'It's awful risky,' he worried. 'I ain't likin' you going down there alone, Boss.'

'How are you going to get them cows to stampede?' the foreman wanted to know.

'You leave it to me,' Mark said. 'Get moving, Pat. You should make it downhill in fifteen minutes. I'm giving you and the boys another fifteen minutes to reach the butte.'

'We'll be there,' promised the Bar H foreman. 'We'll be there with our guns smokin'.'

Mark watched him until he dropped from sight down the storm-made chasm, then again studied the meadow below. The butte in the mouth of the gorge was less than three hundred yards from the camp, a massive pile

163

of granite that had withstood countless years of cloudbursts that had gradually slashed the twisting passage through the hills. It would make ideal cover for the Bar H riders.

He began the precarious descent to the floor of the meadow, careful to avoid starting a slide of loose stones and shale that would attract the attention of the lone rider guarding the herd.

He reached the granite ledge at the base of the cliff and lay behind it for a few moments, recovering his breath and watching the rider now on the opposite side of the bedded cattle. The man's circling course would bring him within a few feet of where he was concealed.

Mark's pulse quickened as he waited, gun in hand. The unsuspecting rider slowly drew nearer, his horse at a plodding walk. He lolled lazily in his saddle, hat pulled low over his eyes against the sun. He reined to a halt in the scant shade thrown by the high ledge behind which Mark crouched, a routine Mark had carefully observed while talking to Pat Race up on the cliff, and which had inspired the action he had in mind.

As he had done before, the rider slid from his saddle and squatted on his heels in the shade, his back to the ledge. Mark got quietly to his feet, peered over the shoulder-high ledge. The man had a flask tilted to his mouth, tobacco and cigarette papers in his free hand. Mark's gun-barrel stuck down at the head less than three feet below him. It was a savagely hard blow. Flask and tobacco sack fell from the man's hands; he sagged limply over on his side. In another moment Mark was dragging the rustler behind the ledge. A brief look told him the man was unconscious. He went quickly to the horse and led the animal behind the higher end of the ledge, from possible view of the tents. He hooked the reins over a projecting splinter of granite and untied the coiled lariat from the saddle. The luckless rider was regaining his senses by the time Mark had him securely tied hand and foot. He gazed up, dawning recognition in his eyes.

'I'm knowin' you,' he mumbled. 'You're that Bar H feller.'

'That's right.' Mark jerked the man's bandanna from his neck. 'I'm tying up your mouth.'

'Listen,' pleaded the dazed rustler. 'Let me git away from here and I'll tell you somethin'.'

Mark hesitated. Time was precious, but the man's sheer fright held his interest. 'Talk fast,' he said, 'and talk low.'

'I'm done with that damn snake, Bett,' the rustler whispered hoarsely. 'He's leavin' my pardner, Pecos, lay in that ravine for the buzzards.'

'It was you and Pecos, on the trail last night?' Mark asked.

'Bett sent us to lay for you,' Rengo said. 'Them other fellers come up with guns smokin', and now Bett is leavin' Pecos lay there for the buzzards.'

'I don't see why I should turn you loose,' Mark said. 'You would have left me lying there for the buzzards.'

'It's worth it to you,' gasped the rustler. 'I'm tellin' you it's Bett wants to kill you, it's Bett who had Cherokee git old Swan in the hotel ... it's Bett who's the boss rustler in these parts. He's a devil and I hate his damn guts.'

Mark glanced at his watch. Pat Race and the outfit were about due at the mouth of the gorge, awaiting his signal.

'I'll talk to you later,' he told the rustler. 'In the meantime I'm making sure you don't do any yelling to your friends.'

He hurriedly secured the bandanna over the man's mouth, holstered his own gun, and carrying Rengo's .45, crawled towards a

166

boulder that afforded cover close to the herd. His luck had held good. No sign of life stirred at the rustler's camp. His brief affair with Rengo had not been observed. He lay for a few moments behind the boulder, studying the cattle. The Bar H steers were at the far side of the herd, clannishly keeping to themselves, most of them lying down. They would be the first to head the stampede for the wide mouth of the canyon on the right. He glanced at his watch again. No use trying to spot the Bar H outfit at the mouth of the gorge. The men would be careful to keep out of sight until the signal which would be the first onrush of the stampeding cattle.

Mark thrust the watch into his pocket. Time was up. He lifted Rengo's gun, flung five quick shots that threw dust on the nearest recumbent steer... In an instant the thing was done, the cattle up in one billowing motion and surging frenziedly towards the canyon. A massive, thunderous tidal wave that swept over the rustlers' camp and horse corral. Anguished yells rose from the debris of scattered tents as tails up, the great herd roared into the canyon, followed by the panicked horses.

Watching from behind his boulder, Mark

saw the surprised rustlers running in circles among the ruins, some of them only partially clad. Horrified shouts and curses mingled with yells from the Bar H men charging down on them from the gorge.

It was more than the rustlers could take. They scattered in all directions, a score and more completely demoralised renegades, some of them limping on bootless feet, a few lying very still in the tangled ruins of the flattened tents. No fight was left in them. They only wanted to get away from there.

Obeying Mark's beckoning wave, the Bar H men swerved towards him.

'We wasn't needin' to fire a shot,' exulted Pat Race. 'You sure lit a fire under 'em, Boss. Won't be no trouble roundin' 'em up for the sheriff.'

Mark shook his head. 'We've no time to waste on them now, Pat. You and the boys keep going after the cattle – push them on to Willow Creek. They won't run far after they hit the hill.'

Pat gazed at him incredulously. 'You mean you're letting them low-down cow-thieves get clean away?'

'They won't get far,' Mark said. 'No horses – their saddle gear smashed, most of them without guns.' He paused, added significantly, 'I'm not turning them over to our sheriff.'

Rusty Hall cantered up with Mark's horse on a lead-rope. His face wore an awed look. 'Couple of fellers layin' back there, dead,' he said. 'I reckon they was too slow gittin' away from them tents.'

'Any of them lying there too hurt to move?' Mark asked.

'I didn't see none,' Rusty replied. 'Some of 'em is crippled all right, but they're still on the run.' He handed the buckskin's tie-rope over to Mark. 'I reckon we done wiped out this rustler's roost for keeps, Boss.'

Mark gestured wearily at the canyon that had swallowed the stampede. 'On your way, Pat. Keep those cattle headed for Willow Creek before they scatter.' He glanced at the ledge that concealed his captive. 'Rusty, you stay with me. I've got a man here for you to herd back to the ranch.'

'So that's how you pulled it off,' admired Pat Race. 'I figgered you must have nabbed that feller we seen ridin' circle.' He swung his horse. 'Come on, boys ... let's get movin'.'

Mark gazed thoughtfully across at the shambles of flattened tents. 'Rusty, take a look over there for any guns they hadn't time to grab when they ran.'

'That's a smart idee.' The cowboy grinned. 'I reckon I'll find plenty. They was some confused when them cows hit 'em.'

By the time Rusty returned with his loot, Mark had Rengo on his horse, hands tied to saddle horn, feet lashed to stirrups.

The rustler's face was ashen. 'Turn me loose,' he begged. 'I done spilled plenty to you, enough to hang Bett and Cherokee and that snake, Slade. I sure deserve a break.'

'I'm leaving it to the Law,' Mark told him grimly. 'The Law has come to San Carlos to stay. You'll have to take your medicine.'

'Damn you,' snarled the renegade. 'I'm wishin' right now that me and Pecos had got you right last night.'

'Shut your trap,' warned Rusty. 'Any more talk and I'll lay my gun across your mouth.' He patted the blanket-wrapped bundle tied to his saddle. 'You was right, Boss. I found me more'n a dozen shootin'-irons them skunks left layin' there.'

'Fine,' Mark handed the rustler's tie-rope to the cowboy. 'We're taking the short-cut up the gorge. We should make it back to the ranch soon after sundown.'

They rode past the wrecked camp. Mark noticed that Rusty had spread blankets over the two dead rustlers, weighting them down with rocks. He threw the cowboy a grateful nod.

'I wasn't likin' them layin' there for the buzzards.' The distant report of a rifle chased the beginnings of an embarrassed grin from Rusty's face. 'Looks like they're gittin' their tails up ag'in now our bunch has dusted away from here.'

They could see the rustlers gathered at the base of the cliff at the far end of the meadow. Mark surmised the rifle shot was nothing more than a defiant gesture. The distance was too great for accurate shooting.

'A lot of 'em is goin' to do some cussin' when they git back to the camp and find their guns gone,' Rusty said complacently.

Mark made no comment. He was thinking the next day or two would see the finish of Reeve Bett's gang of rustlers. He was not sending Sheriff Corter after them. The sheriff was either one of them, or else a great fool, and not to be trusted. U.S. Deputy Marshal Ed Horne would take care of them. They were unable to escape without horses. They would still be in the vicinity and easily rounded up, despite the few who were still armed.

Mark swung the buckskin into the gorge and up the twisting trail. *Sundown – the ranch*

– and Ellen. His heart lifted as he thought of Ellen. Sunshine was at last breaking through the dark clouds.

CHAPTER FOURTEEN

The morning sun was warm on the drawn shades when Ellen Brice lifted her head from the pillows, awakened by a knock on the door. Dismayed to realise she had over-slept, she threw back the covers and swung her feet from the bed. Her talk with Mark had kept her wakeful for long hours before she had finally fallen asleep.

The knock was repeated. *'Señorita!'* Delfina's voice.

'Yes – I'm awake–'

The Mexican girl came into the room, a cup of chocolate on the tray in her hand. 'You 'ave nize sleep, *Señorita,*' she greeted.

'I should have been up hours ago,' Ellen said with a rueful smile. She reached for robe and slippers. 'Thank you for the chocolate, Delfina.'

'Señora Copa say let you sleep long time.' Delfina went to the windows, drew up the shades. She stood for a long moment, gazing at the Mexican leaning indolently against the high patio wall. A high-peaked sombrero,

adorned with a red band, shadowed his face. Cartridge belts criss-crossed his chest and a rifle leaned at his side against the wall. The movement of the window-shades drew his quick look. White teeth glimmered in a smile of recognition.

'Please do pull the curtains,' begged Ellen, and then, curiously, 'Who is he, Delfina? I've not seen him before.'

Delfina hastily drew the curtains. Ellen wondered at the sudden colour in her cheeks. 'He ees Felipe, *Señorita*. Our *Señor* breeng heem an' Ramon from town last night. Felipe an' Ramon ver' brave hombres an' *Señor* Mark 'ave them keep guard in patio while he gone.'

The cup of chocolate almost slipped from Ellen's fingers. She replaced it on the tray. *Mark gone and without a word!* She managed to keep her voice casual. 'Where has Mr Hudson gone, Delfina?'

'*Señor* Mark, 'ave go look for cows rustlers steal from rancho.' The Mexican girl went to the bathroom. 'I feex nize bath for you, *Señorita*.'

Ellen listened dully to the sound of water splashing in the tub. Her wild talk had frightened Mark, destroyed his love. He had not even waited to talk to her father about it.

It was all over between them, or he would not have left her without a word of explanation. She was no longer first in his thoughts. His cattle were more important than Samuel Brice and his daughter.

Perhaps it was the bath that took the tension from Ellen, or more probably it was common sense thinking that began to absorb the shock of Delfina's news about Mark. After all, it was her own fault. She had practically told him there could be nothing more between them. Self-recriminations raced through her mind as she hastily got into her clothes. She was jumping at conclusions that could be all wrong. Mark was a cattleman. It was natural for him to be concerned about his missing steers.

She tiptoed into her father's room. He was propped against the pillows, eyes closed, apparently asleep. The shades were still down and he looked worn and haggard in the dim light. She bent over for a closer look, alarmed by his pallor.

His eyes fluttered open, met her concerned look. 'Is that you, Ellen?'

'I overslept–' She touched his bandaged shoulder. 'How's the arm?'

'Just fine,' Brice said. His eyes closed again.

'Have you had anything to eat?' Ellen asked.

His eyes opened, a faint smile in them. 'Yes – hours ago. Our friends are wonderfully kind.'

Ellen wanted a better look at him. She went to the windows and drew up the shades. Felipe was still in the patio, squatting now on his heels against the wall, a cigarette drooping from lips. Contrition moistened her eyes; she turned back to the bed. Yes, Mark was more than kind. He had gone off chasing cattle and rustlers, but his protecting arms were around her. She could feel their reassuring strength.

'Have you talked with Mark – yet?' Brice asked.

'He's away,' Ellen evaded.

'Yes, Teresa told me when she brought my breakfast. Didn't he tell you he was going?'

'No–' Ellen's finger-tips brushed his cheek. 'You need a shave.'

'You talked with him last night?'

'Yes,' she reluctantly admitted. 'He said nothing you could tell him would change his – his mind.'

'It mustn't change yours, Ellen – if you love him.'

'I do, I do,' Ellen said piteously. 'It's only

fair for him to know *everything* – first.'

'I'll tell him everything when he gets back.' Brice smiled up at her. 'Mark Hudson is a man in every meaning of the word, Ellen. You can believe him when he says nothing can alter his feeling towards you.'

'I must wait for him to decide.' Ellen's chin lifted. 'I won't blame him if he changes his mind.'

'He won't,' Brice said. 'If I could only find Pollett Quin,' he murmured. 'I'd make Quin clear my name if I had to kill him doing it.'

'Don't think about him now,' urged Ellen. 'It's not good for you to worry about him – or me.'

Pollett Quin, alias Reeve Bett, was having a conference in his office with Sheriff Corter and Ed Starkey. Slade was there, an interested listener.

'Don't ask me how I found out,' Bett said. 'Hudson is hiding Brice at his Bar H ranch. The girl, too.' His gleeful look went to Slade. 'It explains why you and Curly couldn't pick up their tracks at the Brice place. Hudson must have got them away during the storm.'

'I reckon that's right,' growled the desperado. 'Whatcha figger to do, Boss.'

Bett's teeth glimmered in his fox-like grin.

'Plenty, and this time I'm doing it legal.'

Sheriff Corter shifted uneasily in his chair. 'You mean you're dragging me into it?' he asked grumpily.

'You're the Law,' Bett reminded him. 'You're swearing in a posse and going out to the Hudson ranch and arrest Brice as a fugitive from justice.'

'I ain't got a warrant,' worried the sheriff. 'I ain't caring to snatch Brice away from Mark Hudson and no warrant to show it's legal.'

'I'll fix up a warrant for you,' Bett said. 'It will be good enough to fool Hudson.'

'Hudson don't fool easy,' grumbled the sheriff.

'What will we do with Brice when we land him in jail?' asked Ed Starkey.

'I think Brice will be fatally shot while resisting arrest,' Bett said significantly. 'Slade will be in the posse and he'll make sure Brice doesn't escape.'

Starkey and the sheriff exchanged startled looks.

'It's murder,' the rancher muttered. 'You leave me out of it, Reeve.'

'Me, too,' grunted the sheriff. His face was pale. 'You're forgetting Mark Hudson. He won't stand for it.'

'You're arresting Hudson, too, for harbouring a criminal,' Bett said smoothly. 'Too bad for him if he's shot for resisting the Law.'

'He'll sure resist,' the sheriff said unhappily. 'I ain't liking this business. I'm quittin'!'

Bett said, softly, 'You're in too deep to quit, Corter.' His penetrating look shifted to the rancher. 'The same goes for you, Ed. You're both in this up to your necks.'

The two men gazed back at him in sullen silence, rebellion, and fear in their eyes. There was menace in the smile he gave them.

'It's more than your ranch at stake, Ed.' His voice was deadly now. 'It's your neck.'

'Damn you!' muttered the rancher. He gestured helplessly. 'I ain't backing out, Reeve, if it comes to a show-down with Hudson.'

'He'll find out sooner or later that you're hand-in-glove with the rustlers. He'll be asking you about the mysterious disappearance of some of your neighbours.'

Starkey glared at him, his face ashen. 'Dammit,' he groaned. 'Shut up. I was livin' decent until you come 'round with your smooth talk.' He reached for the flask on the desk, shakily poured a drink. 'I'm stickin',

179

Reeve. Ain't nothin' else I can do.'

'Too bad for you if you try to cross me up,' Bett warned. His gimlet eyes fastened on the sheriff. 'You've got to stick, too, Corter, or the Law you're supposed to represent will hang you with the rest of us.'

The sheriff's brief rebellion was oozing out of him. His gaunt frame sagged in his chair, defeat, resignation, making a haggard mask of his face.

'I reckon you're right,' he said dully.

'You know the truth about Bill Swan,' Bett said. 'You're an accessory to his murder, Corter.'

The sheriff's hand lifted in a limp gesture of defeat. 'I'm stickin'... Like Ed says, ain't nothin' else I can do.'

'Ed's right.' There was grim warning in Bett's curt response. 'Slade will select the men for your posse,' he continued. 'You'll be the Law out there at Bar H, Corter, but your posse will be my law.'

The sheriff understood the threat. 'I won't stop 'em from finishing the business the way you want,' he said hoarsely. He got out of his chair. 'Are you goin' along with us?'

Bett shook his head. He recoiled from the thought of a second meeting with Samuel Brice who might finally penetrate his disguise, recognise Pollett Quin. Not that recognition would save Brice. Slade and his posse of desperados would take care of Brice. The danger lay in the possibility of others witnessing the fake arrest hearing him exposed as Pollett Quin.

'No need for me to go,' he told the sheriff with a wintry smile. 'I'm leaving it to you and Starkey and Slade.'

Sheriff Corter looked at Starkey and Slade. 'Well, fellers, let's get moving, huh?'

Reeve Bett grinned up at the ceiling. Lucy Swan had cunningly used him to get the information of Brice's whereabouts to the sheriff. Her scheme to get Brice and Ellen out of the house was far more successful than she dreamed. Her ruse had condemned Brice to an early death.

Bett's thoughts lingered admiringly on Lucy Swan. His first opinion of her was strengthened. Her pretty exterior cloaked a hardness that matched his own. She was a cool, calculating little piece, the type of girl he would find useful as a wife. Of course she was in love with Mark Hudson, or her jealousy wouldn't have betrayed his secret. He needn't worry. With Mark Hudson gone, the road to Lucy Swan and the great Swan ranch would be wide and beckoning.

Lucy was doing some thinking, too. She was beginning to hate herself for betraying Mark's secret about the Brices to Reeve Bett. She was remembering her father's distrust of the man. *A cold-blooded, dangerous schemer,* she had once heard Bill Swan say of Reeve Bett. Doubts rankled in her mind. Perhaps her father was right. She recalled the odd look in Reeve Bett's eyes when she told him Mark was harbouring a supposed cow-thief at Bar H.

Fright now laid its clammy hands on her as she thought it over. *A cold-blooded, dangerous schemer* now possessed Mark's secret. Her jealousy had let Mark down, perhaps put his life in peril. She must do something about it, somehow manage to warn Mark.

She leaned over the garden gate opening on the ranch yard where a Flying S man was saddling a colt. She watched him, her thoughts racing. She would send a note to Mark ... send Slim with a note.

'Slim!' she called, 'I want to talk to you.'

The cowboy approached, leading the colt. 'Ma'am?' He looked at her curiously, wondering at her agitation.

Lucy was already discarding the plan. Sending a note was cowardly. She must go in person to the ranch.

'Slim,' she said, 'tell Ben to saddle Cherry for me right away.'

'Ben's down in the pasture, ma'am. If you're in a hurry I'll go saddle the mare myself.'

'I'll be out in the yard in a few minutes.' Lucy sped along the walk and into the house. She felt suddenly lighter of heart. She was doing what her father would have said was the right thing.

CHAPTER FIFTEEN

Fidel Cota reined his horse to a standstill under the shade of a lone oak that overhung the trail. The limp was growing more pronounced and the last stumble warned him that something was seriously wrong. He slid from his saddle for a look. One look was enough to make his heart sink. Brownie had thrown a shoe. A flinty stone had cut and bruised the frog.

Fidel sat down on a boulder and gazed disconsolately at the brown horse. Still twenty miles to go to the town of Hatchita, and here he was, hopelessly stranded with a badly lamed horse. The devil was doing his evil best to keep him from delivering the boss's message to U.S. Deputy Marshal Horne. It was the finish. He had failed his *Señor*.

For long moments he stood there, hand caressing the brown's mane, his eyes roving, taking stock of his surroundings. Relief wiped the despair from his face. The lone, lightning-blasted pine on the ridge to his right was a familiar land-mark. There was a trail there, descending the slope to the long valley that was the old Bar Chain ranch. The owner, Ross Chaine, was *Señor* Mark's friend and would gladly lend him a horse to finish the journey to Hatchita.

Fidel studied the ridge some three hundred yards above him. The brush, the pinon scrub, and the tumbled boulders made the steep climb too slow to attempt. He would save time by following the trail around the shouldering hill to where it intercepted the Bar Chain trail on the summit of the ridge. A half-hour to the summit and another hour down to the Bar Chain ranch-house.

Leading the lamed horse, Fidel started up the trail.

Two men sat on the wide veranda overlooking the Bar Chain ranch yard. The elder of the two, a long, lanky man with a drooping moustache, put down his coffee cup. 'Looks like you have a visitor, Ross,' he said. 'Got a lame horse on his rope.'

Ross Chaine got out of his chair, a blond young giant with eyes startlingly blue in a deeply-tanned face. He said in a surprised voice, 'I know him ... one of Mark Hudson's Mexicans!' His voice lifted in a shout, 'Over here, Fidel!' He resumed his chair. 'It's my guess he wants to borrow a horse.'

'I'm not betting your guess is wrong,' drawled the grizzled-moustached man. 'He's got a mighty lame bronc there.'

A man appeared from the stable, and after a few words with Fidel, led the limping brown to the barn. Fidel made his way to the yard gate into the garden. There was a sag to his shoulders. He was hot and weary from his long walk, and his high-heeled boots were pinching him. Excitement, though, glowed in his eyes as he mounted the veranda steps.

'You look all in, Fidel,' Ross Chaine said. 'Sit down and rest your feet, and have a cup of coffee. Juanita,' he called, 'another pot of coffee.'

'*Gracias.*' Fidel gratefully took the indicated chair. 'My boss does not know you are back from Kansas City, *Señor.*'

He hesitated, looked at the grizzled-moustached man sprawled indolently in his chair, added cautiously, 'I am on my way to Hatchita and need a fresh horse. Brownie lost a shoe and is badly lamed.'

Chaine guessed his reluctance to talk in front of a stranger. He said, 'You don't need to be afraid of him, Fidel. He's U.S. Deputy

Marshal Ed Horne and a good friend of your boss. We came in together last night from Hatchita.'

'*Señor!*' Fidel was on his feet, his weariness forgotten. 'I was riding to Hatchita with a letter from my boss to *Señor* Horne, and now the good saints bring me here to him.' The young Mexican turned an awed look on the deputy marshal. 'We have much trouble at the rancho,' he finished simply.

The deputy marshal held out his hand. 'Let's have it.' He ripped open the envelope Fidel produced from a pocket Teresa had sewn inside his shirt. His brows furrowed as he read the letter.

'I'll say there's trouble at the ranch,' he muttered. He tossed the letter to Ross Chaine, looked at Fidel. 'I'm mighty glad you found me here, young feller.'

A Mexican woman appeared with the called-for coffee. She poured a cup for Fidel. He was not feeling in the mood for coffee at the moment. He was too excited to think of food or drink. To have refused the *Señor's* hospitality would have seemed rude.

Ross Chaine kept cursing as he read the letter. He gazed distractedly at the deputy marshal. 'Bill Swan dead, murdered,' he said in a shocked voice. 'Poor Lucy, and I didn't know a thing about it. A fine friend I am.'

'You were half-way between here and Kansas City when it happened,' U.S. Deputy Marshal Ed Horne reminded him in his quiet voice.

The young rancher looked again at the letter. 'Mark says there have been three attempts to ambush him.' Chaine sprang to his feet. 'I've got to get to Lucy Swan. Anything can happen!'

'Easy does it,' counselled the deputy marshal. 'We can't go off half-cocked, Ross. What do you know about this Reeve Bett he suspects is back of the killings?'

'Not much,' Chaine admitted. 'Hatchita's my town, you know. I've heard talk he about runs San Carlos.'

Horne looked at Fidel, sipping his hot coffee. 'What do you know about him?'

The two men listened, grimly silent, while he gave them a brief account of what he had seen and heard while crouching in the tangle of vines at Bett's office window.

'We've heard enough,' Ross Chaine said impatiently. 'Let's not waste time, Ed.'

Horne shook his head, his expression thoughtful. 'What does this Bett man look like, Fidel?' he asked.

'He is dark, *Señor*, a black beard and

moustache,' Fidel told him.

The deputy marshal shook his head again, disappointedly. 'Doesn't fit,' he muttered.

'He is a little man,' Fidel said hopefully. 'He speaks with an oiled tongue and has the look of a fox.'

Horne's head lifted like a hound that had just caught the scent of an elusive quarry. 'The oiled tongue fits, and the fox look.' Excitement of the chase glowed in the deputy marshal's eyes. 'Do you know a man by the name of Samuel Brice?'

'I've heard of him,' Ross Chaine broke in. 'Owns a small ranch near Mark's Bar H. I've never met him.'

'I haven't told you what brings me down this way,' Horne said. 'I'm looking for Samuel Brice and it was in my mind Mark would know him, put me on his trail.' His keen eyes were questioning the young Mexican. 'Have you seen him around lately, Fidel?'

Panic seized Fidel. The Law was looking for the man rumour said was a stealer of cows, the man who was his *Señor's* friend and now in hiding at the Bar H ranch-house. 'He is not the man with the oiled tongue and the face of a fox,' he evaded.

'You don't need to tell me that,' the

deputy marshal said good-humouredly. 'I'm asking if you've seen him lately.'

'*Si, Señor.*' Fidel spoke cautiously. 'He is a friend of my boss who will tell you about him.'

'Don't want to talk, huh?' Horne's smile was enigmatic. He got out of his chair. 'Ross, I'm needing more than you to help take care of this trouble at Bar H.'

Chaine considered a moment. 'Bar Chain can muster ten men,' he said. 'I'll send a man over to Cameron's Circle C, ask him to meet us with his outfit at Mark's place. More than a score of us all told. You'll be the law with teeth in it, Ed.'

'Fine–' The deputy marshal looked at Fidel. 'How about the Bar H boys? Are they at the ranch?'

'Some of them, *Señor.*' Fidel hesitated, not wanting to speak of the men guarding Brice and his daughter. It seemed that his boss had not mentioned the Brices in his letter and perhaps did not want the lawman to know of their presence at the ranch-house. It was very confusing.

'*Señor* Mark left early this morning for the Willow Creek camp,' Fidel said. 'He went to hunt cattle stolen by rustlers and did not expect you at the ranch until tomorrow night.'

Horne rubbed his chin reflectively. 'We've got to get word to him.'

'I will go, *Señor*,' Fidel offered. 'I know a short-cut from here to the Willow Creek camp.'

The deputy marshal gave him an approving nod. 'Fine! You're a smart boy. Some day you'll be foreman of Bar H.'

'I am a man, *Señor*,' the young Mexican said stiffly. He patted the long-barrelled Colt at his side. '*Señor* Mark has given me the old *Señor's* gun because I am a man.'

'I'll say you are,' Horne said with an amused chuckle. 'All right, Fidel, get youself a fresh bronc and high-tail it to this Willow Creek camp. Tell your boss, if you find him, that I'll be at the ranch by sundown, if not sooner. Tell him I'm bringing plenty of help – the Bar Chain and Circle C outfits.'

'I will find him, *Señor*,' Fidel assured the lawman. In a few minutes, his saddle transferred to a tough-looking blue roan, he rode proudly erect from the yard. There was a great thankfulness in his heart. He had not failed his boss. The good saints were riding with him, stirrup-to-stirrup. Only one thing clung like a troublesome burr to his thoughts. The U.S. Deputy Marshal's interest in Samuel Brice. There could be only one answer. The man his boss had befriended was a hunted criminal. He must warn his boss.

The sun was dipping towards the western peaks when he cut into the Willow Creek trail. He reined the sweat-lathered horse to a standstill in the lengthening shade of a clump of pinons before starting the steep climb over the ridge. The roan had travelled fast and far through the scorching heat of the day and was showing signs of fatigue.

Fidel got down from his saddle. He had ridden a lot of miles since early dawn and was weary, too. They were both entitled to a few minutes' rest. He squatted on his heels against a boulder and leisurely made a cigarette. His idling gaze fastened on a faint haze of dust below the fork of the trail. He gazed at it, heedless of the tobacco spilling from the sack he held over his cigarette paper. Dust meant riders down there, riders descending the slope below him on the trail to the home ranch.

Fidel's gaze came back to where he was resting against the boulder. There were patches of wet earth, lingering remnants of the rain not yet absorbed by the sun because of the shading pinons. Fresh hoof marks showed in the moist patches at his feet. The cigarette paper dropped from his fingers and hastily pushing the sack of tobacco back into shirt pocket, he stooped for a closer look. Three horses, the imprints pointing down trail. The hoof prints of one of the horses was as familiar as the palm of his hand, made by the special plates worn by Mark's buckskin.

Fidel's gaze returned to the haze of dust. His boss was on his way home, two riders with him. His weariness forgotten, the young Mexican leaped into his saddle. The good saints were surely riding with him. If he had missed the significance of those hoof-prints he would have pushed on to the Willow Creek only to find his boss gone.

Rusty Hall, following Mark with the captured outlaw, called out, 'Somebody comin', fast, Boss.'

They pulled off the trail, hands on their guns, saw Fidel tearing around the upper bend. Rusty said in a surprised voice, 'The Mex kid ... I thought he was headed for Hatchita.'

Mark's heart sank. His plan to enlist Ed Horne's help had gone wrong. He could not imagine what had happened. One thing seemed certain, Fidel was bringing bad news or he wouldn't be looking for him. The boy must have run into serious trouble. The horse under him was not Brownie.

Fidel reined the blue roan to a plunging halt. '*Señor.*' His voice was jubilant. 'I have good news–'

Relief wiped the dismay from Mark's face, held him momentarily speechless.

'*El Señor* Marshal Horne already rides for the rancho,' babbled the excited youth.

Mark hardly grasped the import of the words. His surprised look was on the blue roan. 'Where did you get that Bar Chain horse?'

'Brownie lost a shoe and went lame,' Fidel explained. 'The good saints led me to *Señor* Chaine's ranch where he and the deputy marshal were drinking coffee on the gallery.' Fidel could not resist a curious look at Rengo, lashed to his saddle. 'You have found the stolen steers, *Señor?*'

'Yes – yes.' Excitement was growing in Mark. Ed Horne was already on his way to the ranch, that's what Fidel had said, and Ross Chaine was back from his Kansas City trip. The news was good indeed.

'They did not know about *Señor* Swan's murder until the deputy marshal read your letter,' Fidel continued. '*Señor* Chaine was very angry and rides to the rancho with the deputy marshal. He brings his Bar Chain

194

men with him and many men from Cameron's Circle C.'

'Fine!' Mark looked at the young Mexican speculatively. 'Fidel – head for Willow Creek as fast as you can make it. Pat Race is soon due there with a bunch of cattle we took from the rustlers. Tell him I want him at the ranch with all the men he can spare from the camp.'

'*Si, si, Señor–*' Disappointment shadowed Fidel's face. He longed to be at the ranch where there was promise of much excitement. '*Señor–*' He hesitated, glanced doubtfully at the captive outlaw.

Mark guessed there was something on his mind for his private ear. He swung his horse down-trail, his gesture beckoning Fidel to follow.

'What is it?' he asked.

'The big lawman asked questions about *Señor* Brice,' Fidel told him in a low voice. 'I did not tell him he was staying with you at the house.'

'What did he want to know about him,' Mark asked worriedly.

'He did not say.' His boss's perturbation was reviving Fidel's apprehension. Without doubt, the Brice man was wanted by the Law. '*Señor* Horne also asked questions about Reeve Bett. I told him about what I had seen and heard in the yard at the office window. He asked me to describe him and said the black beard and moustache did not fit. I told him the Bett man spoke with an oiled tongue and was small in size. The lawman nodded his head and said, "It fits". I did not understand what he meant.'

'I think I understand what he meant,' Mark said. 'All right, Fidel. You've done a good job today.'

'I hope *Señor* Brice is not in bad trouble,' ventured Fidel.

Mark shrewdly guessed the 'cause of his anxiety. He shook his head. 'Not the trouble you seem to think, Fidel,' he said with an enigmatic smile. 'Don't forget that the Brices are my good friends and I'm standing by them.'

CHAPTER SIXTEEN

Fernando Cota stirred restlessly in his big chair. Petra looked over a shoulder at him from the kettle simmering on the stove. 'You want something?' she asked. 'I am making the fine *puchero* you like for your dinner.'

'It smells good,' he said. His hand lifted in a troubled gesture. 'I smell something that is not good ... I smell danger.'

Teresa Cota overheard him from the kitchen door. She and the cook exchanged frightened looks. When the Old One spoke it was well to take heed. Nevertheless, the housekeeper made an attempt to brush her fears aside.

'Such talk!' she scolded fondly. 'You have been having dreams, Old One.' She hastened to his side. 'A cup of coffee is what you need.'

Fernando's hand lifted again, this time impatiently. 'The danger is close,' he said in his surprisingly deep voice. 'Where is our *Señor?*'

Teresa gazed at him, the alarm back in her

eyes. 'Markito left at dawn for the Willow Creek camp.'

'That is bad,' rumbled Fernando. 'He should be here. The danger is great.'

'Markito said he would not return until tomorrow.' Teresa wrung her hands. 'Your talk frightens me.'

Fernando lifted his massive frame from the chair. 'My boots,' he demanded, 'my guns – the rifle–'

'No, no!' begged the housekeeper. 'You will do yourself harm, Old One.'

'Obey me!' he thundered. 'My boots – my guns!'

Teresa threw up her hands in a helpless gesture of defeat and ran to the small closet sacred to his treasured vaquero equipment. She hurriedly produced the requested boots, the gun-belt with its laden twin holsters – the carbine.

'Where are you going?' she asked as she helped him into the boots.

'The tankhouse tower,' Fernando replied. 'I will keep the watch for this danger.'

Teresa knew the small, heavily-beamed room under the great water tank, used in the old days of marauding Indians as a look-out post. Many a shot had been fired from its loopholes.

'Felipe and Ramon already watch the house,' she said. 'And Markito left men to help guard us – Brasca and Bearcat, old Baldy and Alamo Jones. You are not needed, Old One.'

Fernando stood up in his booted feet, and as before the weight of years seemed gone from his massive shoulders. He proudly faced her. 'Say no more,' he said. 'I serve our young *Señor* as I served the Old *Señor*, his father, when danger stalks the rancho.'

Teresa and Petra watched in silence as the old vaquero stalked from the kitchen, his tread firm, guns in holsters, rifle in hand.

'A man, that one,' the cook said admiringly.

Teresa made no answer. She was fingering the little silver cross she always wore, her lips moving in a whispered prayer.

Fernando hesitated at the tankhouse door. After a moment's thought he continued up the path to the garden gate. He pushed into the yard, lifted a beckoning hand at Alamo Jones standing guard at the granary.

'*Amigo*,' he called.

Alamo sauntered towards him, rifle under an arm, curiosity in his eyes. 'What for your war-paint,' he asked.

'Beeg danger close,' Fernando said. 'I tell

you for keep eye sharp for beeg danger.'

Brasca and Bearcat, watching from the bunkhouse door, exchanged astonished looks.

'The old longhorn is sure on the war-path,' Brasca said in an awed voice. 'He's loaded for b'ar.'

Fernando's gaze rested briefly on the wondering pair at the bunkhouse. 'You tell them I say for keep sharp eye for beeg danger.'

'I sure will, old-timer,' Alamo promised with a good-natured grin.

'*Bueno!* I now go for keep watch in look-out tower.' Stern warning deepened the aged Mexican's voice. 'Beeg danger close to rancho ... we fight for our *Señor.*'

Alamo's gaze followed the aged Mexican thoughtfully as he pushed back through the garden gate. He was no longer inclined to be amused. The old man knew what he was talking about. He spoke with the voice of a prophet, foretelling imminent danger. After all, Fernando was said to be a hundred years old, and perhaps could see into the future, divine the presence of the danger he had warned was close to the ranch.

Stirred to his boot heels, Alamo hastened to impart the startling news to Brasca and Bearcat.

Baldy Bates poked a soap-lathered face through the bunkhouse doorway. 'I reckon if Fernando's talkin' gospel, fellers,' he said. 'If he says he smells trouble I'm bettin' my last chip he's right.' He waved his razor at them. 'Me – I'm cravin' to meet it head on.'

Up in the tankhouse tower, Fernando picked up a long brass telescope that for years had lain on a bench under one of the loopholes. He made the rounds of the loopholes, finally settled on the one overlooking the mesa road to town and the several trails on the lower slopes. It was a powerful glass and his still amazingly keen eyes almost instantly picked up a dust haze on a trail that he knew eventually cut into the road near the avenue. A single rider, coming fast he knew by the lift of the dust.

At intervals the rider disappeared when the trail looped around the bends, each reappearance closer. Fernando suddenly stiffened, muttered an astonished exclamation. The lone rider was a woman – a girl.

He relaxed in his chair for a minute, his seamed face puzzled. He knew every inch of the landscape spread out before him, knew it as no other man in the San Carlos Country knew it. The trail the girl-rider was following came from the direction of the

Swan ranch.

Fernando put his glass on her again, nodded to himself. The Swan girl, and it was obvious she was in great haste, not sparing her horse.

He watched until the trees of the winding avenue hid her. Something very serious must be the cause of her hurried ride, some danger that threatened her, or– The old vaquero's eyes narrowed speculatively. Or it could be she was coming to warn the *Señor* of a peril that threatened him. It *had* to be that, Fernando told himself.

She was suddenly in the yard, Brasca and Tulsa Jim running to her as she reined in at the garden gate.

Fernando listened for a moment to the quick tap of her boot heels as she hurried up the garden walk to the veranda. He resumed his study of the landscape through the brass telescope. Dust again, a long way off, on the town road, a think haze lifting in a long plume. Only a lot of riders could make all that dust.

Fernando laid the telescope on its bench under the loophole. He looked up at the bell, suspended from one of the beams overhead. The Old *Señor* had salvaged it from the ruins of an ancient church destroyed during an India uprising. It had not been tolled in many years, not since the day the young *Señor* was born.

He laid a hand on the dangling rope. It was time to once again pull on it.

Lucy Swan's rush up the veranda steps drew Teresa to the door. She flung it open, amazement widening her eyes.

'*Señorita!*' There was no pleasure in her voice, no welcoming smile.

'Teresa–' Lucy sank on the sofa, breathless with excitement. 'Where is Mark? I must see him immediately.'

'He is not here,' the housekeeper told her stiffly. 'He left early this morning and will not return until tomorrow.' The girl's agitation stirred fright in her. 'What has happened?'

Lucy gazed at her, appalled. *Mark not home!* She felt helpless, undone, sprang to her feet.

'Oh, Teresa – this is dreadful! What shall I do, oh, what shall I do?'

'What has happened?' Increasing anxiety sharpened Teresa's voice. 'Why have you come back to this house?'

Lucy hesitated, reluctant to tell the housekeeper she had betrayed Mark's secret to Reeve Bett. Her confession was for Mark's ears alone. She said, desperately, 'I came to warn Mark the sheriff may be here any minute to arrest Mr Brice.'

The housekeeper drew back, anger in her eyes. 'You told the sheriff,' she accused. 'You – you–' Words failed her.

The Mexican woman's fury seemed to steady Lucy's own quivering nerves. She drew herself up, said quietly, 'We can't waste time talking about it. We must do something ... get Mr Brice away from here.'

Teresa ignored her. 'You wanted the other girl out of the house, so you told the sheriff.'

'There is no time to lose talking about *me*,' Lucy said in the same quiet voice. 'We must get them both away before the sheriff comes.'

'But where?' Teresa gestured helplessly. 'The old man is sick in bed.'

'The sheriff will take him, sick or not, if he finds him here,' Lucy reminded her.

Teresa's keen eyes studied her. This was a new Lucy talking with such authority to her. The spoiled child had given place to a woman. Lucy had grown up.

She said, weakly, 'There is no place where we can hide him.'

'We'll take him to my house,' Lucy said. 'The sheriff will not dream of looking for

Mr Brice in my house.' She thought with repugnance of Reeve Bett. 'Nor anybody else,' she added.

Teresa hesitated. 'It will be difficult to tell them what has happened.'

'I – I'll tell them,' faltered Lucy, her face suddenly pale. She gestured impatiently. 'We must do it before it is too late – before the sheriff comes.'

Teresa lifted a hand. 'Listen!' she said in a hushed voice. 'The bell ... the Old One tolls the bell!'

'What does it mean?' Lucy asked fearfully. 'Why is that bell tolling?'

'It warns that danger comes close,' the Mexican woman told her solemnly. 'It means that it is already too late to move *Señor* Brice from the house.'

Lucy sank dejectedly on the hall sofa and hid her face in her hands. Nor did she see Ellen Brice watching her from the doorway of Samuel Brice's room.

The clamour of the tolling bell reached other ears. Mark heard it with alarm as he rode down trail with Rusty Hall and the captive outlaw. Leaving Rusty to follow with the prisoner, he spurred his horse into a run. There could be only one meaning to the call of the old bell ... Sheriff Corter, riding with his posse to Bar H with a warrant for the arrest of Samuel Brice.

The sheriff heard it, was too engrossed with his unhappy thoughts to more than vaguely wonder. U.S. Deputy Marshal heard it faintly from afar as he followed the Bar H trail with Ross Chaine and a score of hard-bitten riders of the range.

Ross Chaine exclaimed excitedly, 'Listen, Ed! The old Bar H bell!'

'What's it mean?' asked the deputy marshal.

'It means hell is due to break loose at Mark's ranch,' Ross Chaine said.

The deputy marshal said grimly, 'Let's ride.' His horse leaped forward under the touch of spurs. Dust lifted and drifted, made golden haze against the sun now low to the western hills as the men from Circle C and Bar Chain thundered after him.

Sheriff Corter was hating his job, hating the smug, fox-faced little man whose satanic cunning had enmeshed him in the tentacles of treachery and greed and violence.

The sheriff groaned inwardly. He was despairing himself. It had all seemed so trifling at first, shutting his eyes to this and that ... little things at first, then not so little ... burned-out homesteaders and secret terrorism of little ranchers, killings he found it wise to make only a pretence of investigating. Stolen cattle had stocked the ranch that had been his share of the loot resulting from Reeve Bett's ruthless activities. He had prospered, but betrayed the men who had elected him to the office of sheriff. He had lost his honour, lost his soul.

Sheriff Corter glanced at the man riding by his side at the head of the fake posse. One look at Ed Starkey's face was enough. The Lazy S rancher was also suffering the torments of the damned. Ed had been a decent man until he had listened to the evil wiles of the arch-schemer who now held them both captive to his will.

The sheriff stifled a groan, silently cursed himself for a coward. He was letting himself be used as a legal shield for murder – Mark Hudson's murder, Mark, the son of the man who had pinned the Law's silver star on his shirt.

CHAPTER SEVENTEEN

The tolling of the bell drew Ellen to the bedroom door in time to hear Teresa tell Lucy Swan it warned of danger. She closed the door quietly, stood there, a hand on the knob, fighting the terror mounting in her. *Too late to move Señor Brice.* Those were Teresa's words. The bell was warning of imminent danger threatening her father. Lucy Swan was in some way involved. She had collapsed on the sofa.

Her father was calling to her weakly from his bed. 'Ellen – that bell! Why is it ringing?'

She went to him quickly. 'I – I don't know.' She bent over him anxiously, alarmed by his laboured breathing. 'Father – don't try to sit up–' She eased him back on his pillows.

'Sounds like a warning, or something,' Brice said.

'You look so pale,' she worried.

'It's my heart.' Brice closed his eyes. 'I've never told you my heart is not so good.'

'Father!' Ellen held tight to his hand. She longed desperately for Mark.

'It will pass,' Brice said. 'The bell startled me.'

The clamour of the bell hushed, and in the silence Ellen could hear the thump of her own heart. 'I'll send for the doctor.'

'He can't do anything for me.' Brice patted her hand. 'Don't worry ... I'm feeling better already.'

She crossed the room to the door. 'I'll be back in a few minutes,' she promised.

She went through the hall to the wide veranda and down the steps to the tank-house. The door was open. The ground floor, cool, dim, was used as a dairy room. There were pans of milk on a shelf, forming cream for the big churn in one corner. Steep, ladder-like steps led up to the tower.

She could hear voices up there, a woman's voice, a man's deep rumble. Old Fernando ... Teresa!

Ellen's mouth tightened. She went up the steps swiftly, paused in the narrow doorway, breathless, and startled. She had not expected to find Lucy Swan up in the tower with Teresa and Fernando.

There was surprise and dismay in the looks they turned on her. Old Fernando had a long brass telescope in his hands. He muttered something and turned to the loophole at his shoulder.

'*Señorita!*' Teresa hurried to her. 'What is it?'

Ellen glanced up at the bell overhead. 'I heard what you said to Miss Swan when the bell began to ring. 'What – what is this trouble?'

'It is very bad trouble,' Teresa said gravely. 'The Old One sees many riders coming from town and we fear it is the sheriff coming for *Señor* Brice.'

'Oh, no!' Ellen ran to the loophole, reached for the telescope. 'Let me look!'

Fernando surrendered the glass. 'It is the sheriff,' he said. 'He has many men with him, and his friend, Ed Starkey.'

Ellen steadied the long telescope on the sill. The approaching riders were frighteningly near. A few minutes more and they would be in the avenue. One look was enough. She handed the glass back to Fernando and sank on a stool. She felt limp, undone. *The sheriff and a posse coming to arrest her father, carry him off to jail.* It was more than she could bear. It would kill him. She was vaguely aware of Teresa's voice.

'*Señorita* Swan knew the sheriff was coming and hurried from her ranch to warn Markito. When she learned that Markito is not here she wanted to take you both to her home where the sheriff would not think of looking for you.' Teresa gestured sadly. 'She was too late.'

Ellen got to her feet. Her father was lying there, helpless in his bed. She must be with him when the sheriff came. She didn't know what she could do, except plead with the sheriff to leave him alone.

Lucy Swan sensed what was in her mind and was suddenly at her side, her arms around her. 'I'll go down with you,' she said. 'I want to help. We won't let your father be – be taken away.'

Ellen stiffened under the unexpected embrace. The girl wanted to help because she was in love with Mark – wanted to play the heroine for his benefit.

Lucy seemed to read her thoughts. 'Please,' she begged. 'I'm your friend.'

Ellen looked into the lovely, pleading eyes. This was a different Lucy, she suddenly realised. This was not the same Lucy who had left the house that night in a jealous rage. Something had happened.

'Thank you, Lucy–' She spoke tremulously. 'Friends are very precious at this moment. I'll be glad to have you with me.'

She turned to the stairs. Fernando's

excited voice halted her. He had been sweeping the landscape far and wide with the powerful telescope.

'Dust, coming fast down the Willow Creek trail,' boomed the Old One's voice. He swung the telescope to the right. 'Dust, dust, lifting on the Hatchita road ... many riders coming fast!'

Ellen ran again to the loophole and seized the telescope. It was true. A haze of dust on the slope she knew dropped down from Willow Creek, a fast-moving drift that lifted like a golden veil against the last rays of the sun. *Mark,* she prayed. *Mark!* She shifted the glass. More dust over there, the billowing plume lifted by many horses. Her heart lifted too. Friends, of course they were friends – they had to be friends.

Fernando took the telescope from her, placed it on the bench and picked up the rifle leaning against the wall. 'They heard the bell,' he said complacently, '*Si,* they heard the bell.'

'They – they can't get here in time.' Ellen's hope was fading. 'The – the sheriff is almost here.'

Fernando poked his rifle through the loophole. 'We will hold them back, *Señorita.* Brasca and the others are on the watch, and

I can still shoot straight in defence of the rancho.' He looked around at Teresa. 'Pull on the rope – let them hear the bell ring again.'

Teresa grasped the dangling rope and began to pull, and as the ancient bell tolled its summons, Ellen and Lucy fled down the narrow stairs.

The deep-toned clamour of the bell startled Sheriff Corter. He reined his horse, bringing the posse to a plunging halt midway down the avenue. Slade spurred close to his side, gun in hand.

'What for you stoppin'?' he asked angrily.

'That damn bell again,' muttered the sheriff. 'Looks like they're expecting us.'

'What the hell,' growled the renegade chief. 'The Bar H outfit is miles away, up at Willow Creek. Won't be more than two-three used-up mossyhorns home.'

'Mossyhorns can be plenty sharp,' Ed Starkey said sourly. He was not liking the gun in the hand of the posseman who had surged alongside him.

'Quit stallin',' rasped Slade. 'You're ridin' into that yard and puttin' handcuffs on Hudson and Brice. You're sheriff and that makes it legal.'

'As sheriff, it's my duty to see 'em safe to jail,' Corter reminded him curtly.

His attempt to reassert his official authority drew contemptuous grins from the hard-
visaged riders interestedly listening to the
argument.

'All you've got to do is serve them warrants,' retorted Slade. 'We'll finish the rest of
the job the way the boss said.' He gestured
with his gun. 'Get moving... We want away
from here before sundown.'

'Damn you,' muttered the sheriff. He
prodded his horse into a lope. The posse
swung into formation behind him.

The yard gate was closed, fastened with a
heavy chain. One of the riders dismounted
and examined the padlock.

'Use your gun on it,' Slade suggested.

'Cain't git at it good from this side,' the
man said. He drew his gun, climbed the
gate, leaned over the top rail and aimed the
.45 at the heavy padlock below him. A rifle
shot shattered the momentary stillness there
as the waiting posse watched him. The man
uttered a pained yell.

He scrambled down, the gun slipping
from a bullet-smashed hand.

Another rifle bullet whined viciously overhead. In a moment the horses were milling
and plunging as the panicked renegades
attempted to swing away from the gate. The

wounded man tried to grasp the dangling reins of his horse with his good hand, stumbled and fell. A shod hoof of the rearing animal came down with a sickening impact on his skull, left him a motionless, crumpled heap on the ground.

Slade's furious shouts halted the stampeded posse around the first nearby bend where the trees hid them from view of the deadly marksman. He had not for a moment kept his eyes off the sheriff and Ed Starkey.

He waggled his gun at the sheriff. 'Get back there to the gate ... tell 'em you're the sheriff ... tell 'em it's the Law wants in.'

'I ain't likin' it,' muttered Corter. 'Somebody's put Hudson wise to us.'

'Get goin',' growled Slade. 'I'll be watchin' you, so don't try to give us the slip. There's a four-strand barbed wire fence both sides of us and you can't go through that gate.'

Sheriff Corter reluctantly rode back to the gate, holding his hand high in the sign of peace. No sign of life there in the big yard. He was not fooled. He knew that vigilant eyes were watching him.

He reined his snorting horse past the dead man and halted close to the gate, his spine tingling. Any instant might bring a bullet smashing the life from him.

215

'I'm the sheriff!' he shouted. 'I'm the Law!'

The clanging of the bell suddenly hushed.

'I'm here to serve a warrant on Samuel Brice, known to be hiding in the house. In the Law's name, let me in peaceable.'

'Your brand of law ain't got authority here, Corter,' a harsh voice answered from somewhere in the barn. Alamo Jones, the sheriff recognised. 'We got plenty fellers poster 'round,' warned Alamo. 'There'll be lead flyin' if you make another try at that gate.'

'You can't buck the Law,' argued the sheriff, a lack of conviction in his voice. 'Open up.'

His answer was a rifle shot, the savage ping of a bullet in the gate-post. Sheriff Corter swung his horse hastily away, not before he noticed the gunsmoke curling from the tankhouse tower. The marksman up there would not miss his next shot.

Slade regarded the frustrated sheriff sourly as he rejoined the group. 'I heard the talk,' he said. 'Only thing we can do is wait until dark. We got to figger some way to sneak in on 'em.'

One of the riders stirred uneasily in his saddle. 'Listen!' he said.

The bell was silent now, and in the twilight's stillness the throbbing murmur that reached them from beyond the avenue trees was unmistakable. The drumming hoof-beats of horses.

'Comin' fast,' muttered Slade. 'A lot of 'em!'

'Headin' for the avenue,' one of the posse said uneasily. 'Let's get out of here, before we're boxed in. That locked gate and the bob wires on both sides of us makes this place a damn trap.'

Disregarding Slade's profane protests, the posse swung their horses in a retreat down the avenue. The renegade chief spurred after them, herding the sheriff and Starkey along with him.

Mark was riding up the ravine between the mesa and the barn when Fernando fired his first shot from the tankhouse. He left his horse tied to the dead stump of greasewood and crawled up the steep slope in time to see the posse's hurried scramble to get away from the gate. He lay there, concealed behind a boulder, watched them reassemble in the first bend of the avenue. The scene between the sheriff and the tall, swarthy man he instinctively guessed was Slade, was enough to tell him the story. Sheriff Corter was being forced to arrest Brice, carry him off to jail, or to a worse fate. Thanks to the vigilance of the men left on guard the first attempt had been foiled.

From where he crouched, he could see the gate, witnessed the reluctant sheriff's second attempt, heard Alamo's derisive answer to the demand for admittance in the name of the law. He was hearing, too, the swelling muffled thunder of fast-riding horsemen approaching the avenue. U.S. Deputy Marshal Horne and the Bar Chain and Circle C men. Thanks to Fidel Cota the real law was in action. Horne was keeping his word to reach the ranch by sundown. Corter and his fake posse were in danger of being trapped in the avenue unless they got away from there in a hurry. No way of escape because of the high barbed-wire fence on either side, and behind them, the locked gate – the ready rifles of the men guarding it. The only way out was down the avenue, to scatter in the chaparral before Horne and his riders reached the entrance.

The alarmed renegades were already spurring their horses into a run. Mark lifted his rifle. He must slow them down, give Horne time to block the escape. His first shot tumbled the leading rider from his saddle. He continued to pull the trigger. The fleeing desperados reined to a plunging halt, confused by the unexpected hail of bullets coming from beyond the fence. Some of them abandoned their horses and sought cover behind the giant cottonwoods and oaks that lined the avenue. A few began firing wildly in the direction of the boulder where Mark crouched.

The situation was more than Ed Starkey could take. 'I'm gettin' away from here!' he shouted hoarsely. 'To hell with you, Slade!' He swung his horse towards the gate, spurs gouging. Slade coolly shot him in the head.

The rustler jumped his horse close to the sheriff whose stunned gaze was on the slain Lazy S rancher. Shock held him in a momentary stupor.

'Damn you!' shouted Slade. 'You sent word we were comin' ... led us into a trap!'

Sheriff Corter came out of his trance, as Slade's gun lifted. With his old-time lightning reach, his own gun was in his hand. The two shots blended like one. Slade slumped forward, a surprised look in his eyes, pitched lifeless from his saddle.

The sheriff gazed down at him, a hand clutching saddlehorn. The smoking .45 slipped from his fingers, his long, gaunt frame sagging lower and lower in the saddle as his horse followed the slain friend's riderless horse towards the gate.

Ed Horne and his deputies were riding hard for the avenue now, hastened by the gunfire. They roared through the entrance. A few of the panic-stricken posse tried to escape by crawling under the barbed wires, quickly changed their minds when Brasca and Bearcat opened fire on them from the grove of trees near the house.

Their leader was dead, another of them was a hoof-mangled corpse near the gate. Three others were more or less seriously wounded, including the man Mark's first bullet had knocked from his saddle. Resistance drained out of them like water from a staved-in barrel. Sullen, submissive, they dropped their guns, lifted hands in the sign of surrender.

U.S. Deputy Marshal Horne eyed the group of nearly a score of prisoners with grim satisfaction. There were faces among them he recognised, men long wanted by the law. He got down from his saddle and joined Mark and Ross Chaine who were bending over Sheriff Corter, lying close to the dead rustler chief. Life still lingered in the sheriff and there was recognition in his dimming eyes as he looked up at Mark.

'Get Reeve Bett,' he whispered. 'It was

him fixed for Swan to be killed.' The sheriff's fingers went feebly to the silver star pinned to his shirt. 'Your dad put it there, Mark. You take it ... I ain't wearin' it no more.' He was suddenly silent, something like peace smoothing his haggard face.

Mark straightened up, looked grimly at Horne and Ross Chaine. 'You heard what he said about Bill Swan.'

Ross Chaine said violently. 'I'm getting his murderer. Anything might happen to Lucy, with him still loose.'

Brasca and Bearcat, climbing under the barbed wire fence, overhead him. 'The Swan gal is over to the house,' Brasca said. 'Come in this evenin'.'

Ross Chaine was not waiting to hear more. He ran to his horse. Mark watched him go, something like relief in his eyes. Plenty of help and comfort for Lucy now. He turned to the deputy marshal.

'Why are you looking for Samuel Brice, Ed?' he asked.

'If my guess is right, the Mexican kid told you,' Horne said with a glimmer of a smile.

'That's right–'

'Do you know where I can find Brice?'

'Tell me first what you want with him,' insisted Mark.

'I don't want him for anything.' The deputy marshal tapped his breast pocket. 'I only want to hand him some papers proving him innocent of a crime.'

Mark was silent for a long moment. *Ellen ... Ellen ... it's all right!* Aloud, he said simply, 'Brice is staying with me, Ed.'

'Fine–' The deputy marshal's voice showed no surprise. 'I guessed as much from the way your Fidel shied away from my questions about him.' He turned to his horse, waited while Mark gave Brasca some instructions about Corter's remains.

'I'll git the wagon,' the cowboy said. 'Leave it to me and Bearcat, Boss. We'll haul in them other fellers, too.'

The U.S. Deputy Marshal continued his story as the two rode towards the gate, now wide open. 'This Pollett Quin I'm looking for was cashier in a bank ... swindled the bank out of a lot of loot ... fixed things so the bank's president was accused and sent to prison. The president was Samuel Brice,' the deputy marshal added laconically.

'Pollett Quin–' Mark shook his head. 'I never heard of him.'

The deputy marshal gave him a sly look. 'Your Fidel tells me that Reeve Bett has an oiled tongue and looks like a fox.'

'That describes him,' Mark said.

'The only trouble is – Quin is a blond and was clean shaven when last seen. Fidel says Bett is dark and wears a beard.'

'I always thought he used dye,' Mark said. 'He's your Pollett Quin, all right, Ed. It explains his attempt to kill Brice, and me, too. He wouldn't know how much Brice had told me of his troubles ... would want me out of the way, too.'

The deputy marshal nodded. 'We'll have a little talk with Mr Reeve Bett tonight,' he said.

They were through the gate now, and Mark hardly heard him. He was thinking of Ellen, waiting there in the house.

CHAPTER EIGHTEEN

Reeve Bett stood in the doorway of his office, speculative gaze on the flaming sunset. Those crimson clouds slowly lifting above the peaks might bring another rain in a day or two. Much had happened since the first storm of four days ago had broken the drought. About this time another kind of storm was wreaking havoc at the Hudson farm, a destructive storm of violence and death, a storm of his own contriving.

The street was unusually quiet. It would be, with Slade and his friends away. Only a few riders in town from outlying ranches. Business would be dull at the Roundup. Much celebration, though, later, when Corter and the posse returned. The drinks would be on the house, he had promised Slade.

Bett closed his office door and started across the street towards the hotel. He might as well have his dinner while awaiting the sheriff's return.

Sol Kramer stood in the doorway of his store, looking down the street for the delayed stage which came in twice a week from Hatchita. Bett remembered the promise to himself to have a talk with Sol about his offer to buy him out. He changed his direction, climbed the steps to the high porch. The storekeeper, who was also the town's postmaster, gave him a stiff nod.

'The stage is late again,' Bett said, his smile urbane.

'Yah – so I wait to get out the mail.'

'How about my offer?' Bett asked.

'No, no–' Kramer shook his head. 'Your offer not good for me.'

'Don't be a fool,' Bett said. 'I can start a new store, much finer than yours ... get the post office away from you.'

Fright looked from Kramer's bulging eyes. 'I will be ruined!'

'You'll sell out to me, or you'll be sorry,' Bett told him suavely. 'Think it over, Sol, and make the answer yes. Tomorrow noon is the deadline.' The soft purr was suddenly gone from his voice. 'Accidents happen to people who say *no* to me.'

The storekeeper watched him go, hate, a growing fear in his eyes. With a hopeless gesture he turned into the store, despair and defeat in the dejected sag of his shoulders.

The stars were out when Bett crossed the

street back to his office. A man lurched from the swing-doors of the Roundup Saloon and hurried to overtake him. Bett halted, hand on the latch and turned his head in a surprised look at him.

'I got bad news, Boss,' Gus Silver said dejectedly.

A hint of panic looked from Bett's eyes as he studied the man, noted his weariness, the dusty, brush-torn clothes. He pushed into the office, Gus followed, sank with a groan into a chair and tenderly rubbed a red gash in his arm from which hung the remnants of his shirt sleeve. 'Catsclaw got me when I was chasin' my bronc,' he said glumly. 'Clawed the hide of my leg, too.' He rubbed a blood-stained thigh. 'I'm all in,' he finished.

'What are you talking about?' demanded Bett impatiently.

'The Bar H fellers got the cows away from us,' Gus said. 'It was hell, Boss ... plain hell.'

'I'm asking you what happened?' almost shouted Bett. 'Where's Rengo?'

'I ain't knowin' where Rengo is. He was ridin' circle when the stampede bust over the camp.'

Sweat beaded Reeve Bett's face as he listened to the man's laconic account of the terror that had wiped out the rustlers.

'Run off our broncs, too,' the rustler told him. 'I managed to ketch me one that got tangled up in that damn catsclaw. The other fellers is holed up some place waitin' for me to fetch 'em broncs from town, and any help you can send 'em. Slade and the rest of the outfit.'

Bett spoke with an effort. 'They're all away,' he croaked.

Gus Silver looked at him uneasily. He had never seen such malignance in a man's eyes. *Looks like a coiled rattler.* His hand shifted to the gun on his hip. He got to his feet. He had heard of the boss's maniacal rages. 'Well, I done all I can ... reckon I'll turn in.'

Bett watched him go in stony-faced silence. He seemed to be visibly shrinking in the big desk chair. Fear was gripping him, squeezing his spine with icy fingers. *The rustler camp destroyed ... Mark Hudson's work... He would not be at the ranch house when Corter's posse arrived on murder bent. Mark Hudson was still alive!*

Bett reached a shaky hand to the desk drawer. He pulled it open, stared dully at the little derringer he always kept there. He took it out, examined it, thrust it inside his coat pocket. He reached into the drawer again for the flask of whisky. He hated the stuff, but a drink would take the limpness out of him, put life into his numbed brain. He downed a stiff one, leaned back in his chair, conscious of a warming glow that gradually settled his shocked nerves.

Footsteps, the scrape of spurs on the planked sidewalk, suddenly held him rigid. Somebody was at the door he had forgotten to lock when Gus left. He had been too dazed to think of it.

Bett arose from his chair. The sheriff, of course, back in town with the posse. He would have news. There was a chance Hudson had been home when the sheriff arrived with the warrants.

The thoughts raced through his mind even as the door was flung open. Bett froze in his tracks. Not the sheriff, framed there against the moonlight. Mark Hudson, gun in hand, armed men crowding at his back.

'You seemed surprised to see us,' Mark said.

Bett hardly heard him. His stricken gaze was on the riders passing up the street. The bright moonlight was on them. The posse was back in town, weary, dejected men, hands bound to saddle-horns, armed riders herding them along.

'Yes,' Mark said, his smile bleak. 'They're

on the way to jail ... those of them left alive. Corter and Slade aren't with them. They're dead, Bett.'

Bett found his voice as he backed away from the menacing gun in the hand of the man he had reason to fear. 'I – I don't know what you're talking about.' He fell limply into his chair, attempting to bluster. 'This is an outrage ... forcing your way into my office.'

'You know why we're here,' Mark said. 'We found those fake warrants in Corter's pocket. He talked before he died.'

'I don't know what you're talking about,' insisted Bett.

'Cherokee has talked, too,' Mark went on. 'His confession implicates you in the murder of Bill Swan, and the attempt to murder Brice and me.'

'They – they're damn liars!' Bett shouted. 'I'm a respectable citizen! You can't take the word of such border scum against mine!'

'Rengo has confessed, too,' Mark continued relentlessly. 'Rengo says you're the boss of the rustler gang.'

'Lies!' croaked Bett. 'Lies!'

'Rengo didn't like you leaving his pal, Pecos, for the buzzards, the night you sent them to ambush me.' Mark gestured at a tall man with a grizzled moustache. 'Meet U.S.

229

Deputy Marshal Horne. He wants to talk to you.'

'That's right,' Horne said softly. 'You've changed your appearance a lot. Mr Pollett Quin ... dyed your hair black and grown a beard and moustache.'

Bett shrank back in his chair, horrified gaze on the quiet-spoken deputy marshal. 'Pollett Quin!' His voice was a hoarse whisper. 'I've never heard of him.'

The deputy marshal's face hardened. 'Out of your chair, mister. I'm taking a look at that cache under your desk.'

'Cache? There's no cache under my desk.'

'Get up!' Horne said harshly.

Bett reluctantly arose, stood aside, face ashen, while Mark stooped and pulled the rug from under the desk. In another moment he had the floor-board out.

A man's awed voice broke the brief stillness that followed.

'Sakes!' muttered Brasca. 'I reckon there's most a hundred thousand dollars gold cached in that hole.'

Mark wasn't interested in the gold. He was rummaging through the neat piles of large envelopes, deeds, mortgages, an envelope containing Santa Fe and Albuquerque bank books. He showed Horne a recently-dated deed. 'Saval's deed for his hotel,' he said. 'The one Bill Swan claimed was a forgery, which was why he was murdered.'

He dug out another envelope, ripped it open and extracted a yellowed newspaper clipping. 'Here's your proof, Ed,' he said.

'The bank affair.' His tone was grim. 'Pollett Quin's picture.' His look went to Reeve Bett. 'All right, Pollett Quin, alias Reeve Bett. You're wanted for that old murder you tried to pin on Samuel Brice.'

The attention of most of the other men was still rooted on the stacks of gold in the cache. Reeve Bett spun on his heels and fled for the rear door. Reaching in his pocket for the derringer, he jerked the door open, collided against a man standing on the step. The little pistol exploded in his hand as the impact knocked him sprawling to the ground.

The man, rifle in lowered hand, gazed down at him from the high step, turned his head in a look at Mark and the deputy marshal halting in the doorway.

'Killed hissel with his own gun,' Alamo said in an awed voice. 'Bumped me so hard he knocked the gun ag'in his heart.'

Mark and Horne leaped down the steps, bent over the prostrate body. Horne straightened up. 'He's dead, all right,' he said regretfully. 'I'd have liked to turn him over to the hangman.'

'I'm leaving the rest of it to you,' Mark told the deputy marshal. 'The money in the cache – the papers.'

'I'll take care of things,' Horne promised. 'You'll be wanting to get back to the ranch, tell Brice his troubles are over.'

'You've guessed it,' Mark said, thinking of Ellen. Impatient to be with her hastened his step.

He almost collided with Jim Stagg at the street door. The old liveryman grasped his arm. Mark had never seen him so excited.

'All over, son, huh?'

'All over,' Mark assured him.

'The jail is sure crowded with hang-tree fruit,' Jim Stagg said in a satisfied voice.

'It's going to be more crowded when Horne gathers the bunch we left on foot in the Devil's Hideout.' Mark slapped his old friend on the shoulder. 'I'm on the run, Jim... Want to get back to the ranch.'

The liveryman gave him a shrewd look. 'You'll be some late with the news. Fidel is already headin' there on the jump.'

Mark suppressed his momentary disappointment. Fidel Cota had earned the right to be the bearer of glad tidings. His loyalty and courage had helped tear the mask from a murderer. No need for haste now. Let Fidel have his big moment.

Mark was near the Swan ranch turn-off when the two riders drifted into view through the moonlight. A man and a woman, their horses side by side, moving at a leisurely walk. Ross Chaine and Lucy Swan, much engrossed with each other.

Mark reined in at the turn-off. Even in that elusive moonlight he could read the story in their faces as they approached.

'Mark!' cried Lucy. 'We met Fidel.'

'He told you?'

'Yes, yes–' She gazed up at him in a way that made him wonder. 'That – that awful man!'

'It's all over,' Mark said.

'I would never, never have forgiven myself if – if–' Her voice broke.

'You've been wonderful,' Mark said. 'Ellen told me how you came to help ... warn them about the sheriff.'

'Was that all she told you?' asked Lucy.

'She told me she thinks you are the most wonderful girl in the world and the bravest,' Mark replied. He was not going to admit that Teresa had told him about the betrayal of his secret.

233

'I've been telling her the same thing,' Ross Chaine said.

'Ross is taking me home,' Lucy broke in confusedly.

Mark's warm smile embraced them both. 'I know you are going to be very, very happy – you two.'

'That's right!' Ross Chaine leaned over, slipped an arm around the girl's waist. 'We know it, too, don't we Lucy?'

'Yes–' Lucy gave him a starry-eyed look. 'Yes, Ross. We know – now.'

Mark watched them ride through the moonlit night, a vast content in his heart, also an impelling urge to be on his way.

Fidel was the first to see him, long telescope levelled through the tower loophole. Bright moonlight silvered the road where it made its sweep for the avenue. No mistaking that lone rider on the fast-moving horse.

Teresa threw up her hands. *The senorita!* She must hurry to her with the big news.

The impatient knock on her bedroom door drew Ellen from her chair with a startled exclamation.

Teresa's beaming face peered through the door. 'He comes!' she said.

'Oh!' Ellen's breath quickened. 'I – I must go to him!' She ran into the hall as Teresa held the door wide open.

Teresa's beaming look went to Brice in the arm chair. He was fully dressed now, his arm in a neat sling, the haggard lines gone from his face.

'Listen!' she said. 'The Old One pulls on the bell rope.'

'What does it mean?' asked Ellen's father. 'It's a merry peal,' he added.

'It means the old rancho will very soon have a new mistress,' Teresa Cota told him happily. 'It means that in due time the old bell will ring again for a new-born son as it rang at Markito's birth.'

Mark saw her as he rode into the moonlit yard. In a moment he was down from his saddle and running to her. With a little cry Ellen ran into his arms.

The publishers hope that this book has given you enjoyable reading. Large Print Books are especially designed to be as easy to see and hold as possible. If you wish a complete list of our books please ask at your local library or write directly to:

The Golden West Large Print Books
Magna House, Long Preston,
Skipton, North Yorkshire.
BD23 4ND

This Large Print Book, for people
who cannot read normal print,
is published under the auspices of

THE ULVERSCROFT FOUNDATION